Vanikin in the Underworld

Vanikin in the Underworld

Mark Gullick

Mark Gullick is a philosopher (Ph.D. University of Sussex) who writes on English politics and culture for American magazines.

He was born in London in the early 1960s, and he currently resides in Central America.

FALLING MARBLES PRESS
Marble Falls, Texas
www.fallingmarbles.com

"Cascading Worth, One Work at a Time"

Eurydice trod on a serpent as she fled, and died of its bite. But Orpheus boldly descended into Hades, hoping to fetch her back...
Robert Graves, "The Greek Myths"

Then you are not one of us? You are well, you are but a guest here, like Odysseus in the kingdom of the shades? You are bold indeed, thus to descend into these depths peopled by the vacant and the idle dead...

Descend, Herr Settembrini? I protest. I have climbed some five thousand feet to get here.
Thomas Mann, "The Magic Mountain"

Contents

FOREWORD TO THE NOVEL　　15
Stephen Paul Foster

ONE　　23
Inappropriate Teaching Methods

TWO　　30
The Fall of Mulciber

THREE　　37
Estrella and the Arriviste

FOUR　　44
In the TV Room

FIVE　　51
Magda and the Measuring Man

SIX　　58
Preparations for a Royal Visit

SEVEN　　65
Queen and Consort

EIGHT 72
I am Everywhere Else

NINE 79
Breakfast of Champions

TEN 86
Time and the Maiden

ELEVEN 93
The Wonders of the Invisible World

TWELVE 100
The Life and Times of Jimmy-Shawn Pallis

THIRTEEN 107
School for Vandals

FOURTEEN 115
Measure for Measure

FIFTEEN 122
The Follies of Pygmalion

SIXTEEN 129
In the Antechamber

SEVENTEEN 137
Europa After the Rain

EIGHTEEN   144

Dinner with Estrella

NINETEEN   153

Of First and Last Editions

TWENTY   160

Let the Games Begin

TWENTY-ONE   167

Entry of the Gladiators

TWENTY-TWO   174

Term Time

TWENTY-THREE   181

A New Printing

TWENTY-FOUR   189

The Book of the Dead

TWENTY-FIVE   196

The Dinner Party

FOREWORD TO THE NOVEL

by Stephen Paul Foster

Mark Gullick is a philosopher, and having read a number of his philosophical writings, I can say with confidence that they make for the best kind of philosophical reading. Mr. Gullick has turned his sights to fiction, a novel, *Vanikin in the Underworld*. I feel compelled to recommend it to serious readers of both fiction and non-fiction—strongly compelled. Fiction lovers will be drawn to the droll self-mockery of the narrator and delight in the masterful outpouring of sardonic, coruscating wit that assaults contemporary fashions, fads, and politically-correct fetishes. The wild metaphors and caustic similes come flying off the pages with a speed and volume of June bugs hitting your windshield on a warm summer night. Historians, philosophers, and scholars of various persuasions will be enviously struck by the author's range of erudition, which he puts to use—often with hilarity—in eviscerating the preposterous, bloated fraud that the "modern" university has become. The book is both uproariously funny and deeply sad. I must add: It is acutely descriptive of the sewer that popular culture has slid into. One of the many ironies that emerges for the reader is that the underworld in which Vanikin finds himself turns out to be a more decent and honest place than the overworld that ejected him.

The novel's central character and narrator, Harry Vanikin, begins with a ghastly telling of his precipitous fall from a high perch of professorial acclaim as the result of a feminist-launched, Stalinist-style public purge. His book, the *Decadent Turn*, was written for fellow scholars as "a critical examination of academic theory from the Renaissance to the present day." It was the spark that ignited the short fuses of the cognitively-limited fanatics who call the shots at what's left of the academy. "[T]he book was remade as a white supremacist tract, a racist screed, a tool of oppression and every other label pulled from the semantic box of tricks a certain type of academic has at their disposal."

With the purge completed, the "disgraced" professor finds himself entombed in a crummy apartment in an even crummier housing project somewhere in London where you won't find the tourists. In this bleak underworld where he has been deposited after a bout of temporary insanity, our Lazarus, ex-philosophy professor, is attended to by a cast of characters from a sociological and ethnic demographic appropriate to the ironically-named "Europa House." Built in the late 1960s, it "resembles a hybrid of an East German tax office and a giant lock-up by a ring road"—perhaps with an East German-style *Lebensfreude,* the kind that made the attempt to leave worth the risk of getting shot.

Vanikin's defenestration has turned him agoraphobic. For seven years, he blots out the changes from night to day and rattles around inside his cage reflecting on the train wreck of a society—the "overworld" out of which he has been cast—that makes public enemies out of truth-tellers, philosophers who dare to philosophize:

"In a world where pinheaded advertising executives spend Third-World-economy-sized amounts selling children plastic and rubber shoes endorsed by multi-millionaire hoodlums who made their own fortunes braying about violent sex acts and ballistic weapons, my teaching methods were inappropriate?"

Here in the United States, the black "multi-millionaire hoodlums" routinely beat up their girlfriends and denounce the white racist fans who make them rich in limited vocabularies of which "motherfucker" does the heavy lifting. But Professor Vanikin committed the "inappropriate." "Inappropriate" continues to be one of my favorite weasel-words favored by teacher-ed establishment types, human resources staffers, and effeminate scolds. Amorphous and protean, it is typically retrieved by cowardly duff-sitters behind their administrative desks to complete the banishment of unsuspecting offenders of recently-invented politically-incorrect crimes and misdemeanors, abandoning innocents to be mauled by howling, primitive mobs.

Harry also expounds on the abnormalities and aberrancies of his fellow refuges in the "project." Declan, for example: "a young man habitually embalmed in cheap Scotch and tax-funded barbiturates." Then there is the resident caretaker of Europa House, Craig McCerrow: "[He] is one of the most frightening of God's creations. God, or whoever runs this spiteful orb." God must have outsourced the management of this Bedlam barracks to one of his surly apparatchiks. Yes, Craig makes a very deep impression on the depressed Professor Vanikin. "To see…his sleeveless shirt showing enough of the hinterland of his squamously illustrated body to indicate his likely passage through life thus far, is to see a type of hell." Well, Sartre did say in *No Exit*: "*L'enfer, c'est les autres.*"

Declan, Craig, and an assortment of Vanikin's other dysfunctional—and occasionally criminally-inclined—neighbors make their way in and out of Harry's domicile on various missions that result in black comedic exchanges for the reader. Here, for example, is Harry attempting to allay the suspicions of a lady friend, Estrella, about a new resident who has few possessions in his apartment:

"Perhaps, Estrella, I want to say, he is uncluttered by the endless inventory of the modern. Maybe he eschews the ranks and files of supermarket detritus. Perhaps he's a Buddhist, with a mat and a bowl. Estrella, though, I can see, wants him to be a serial killer, an MI5 intelligence agent, a fugitive from the law, a racist."

Preoccupied with his prison cuisine, Harry describes one such repast in excruciating detail:

"Lunch is a modest affair: corned beef and a puffy white roll liberally smeared in a butter substitute of the yellow colour found in a child's paint-box, followed by tinned pineapple rings, stacked neatly in their alloy cylinder on top of one another like tiny vinyl records, and swimming in a sweet syrup flecked with pulp. Is it a coincidence that the rise of the tin coincided with the onset of nuclear armaments? How could you prepare for Armageddon and a barren nuclear winter with fresh food? The atom bomb versus the tin."

After recoiling from this psychedelic picture and deferring my preparation for lunch, I couldn't help but think of this culinary rendition as a kind of Balzac moment where artful, painstaking description somehow turns into insights that are penetrating, interesting, and striking.

Early in the narration, however, the reader grasps that beneath Vanikin's unleashed agonizing cascade of his quotidian miseries, what is unfolding is actually a love story. Check that, several love stories.

Vanikin is, above all, a lover. The love of his life is philosophy, since his earliest years. Not the shriveled-up philosophy we know today as that dried-out husk of a specialty taught in academic departments by the uninspiring offspring of technicians like Harvard's John Rawls or post-modern, word-salad quacks like Berkeley's Judith Butler. Vanikin's embrace of philosophy is as a polymath, an all-consuming attempt to grasp reality as it manifests itself in the full range of human experience, the kind of philosophy given to the world by Plato and Aristotle, Hume and Kant—none of whom, by the way, worried about "inappropriate."

This account of his love of philosophy also comes with a lament for its fate in the post-modern world. In a hilarious metaphorical riff with "divorce" as the vehicle image, Vanikin captures the post-Enlightenment descent of philosophy from its long reign over the quest for knowing into a hobby for navel-gazers and a comfortable perch for academic backbenchers.

Here, then, is the funniest and most sagacious passage in the novel:

"When it became increasingly apparent, post-

Enlightenment, that most of what philosophy was doing was actually fledgling science, the resulting schism, had it been framed in the terms of a modern divorce, meant that science got the kids, the house, the car, and the pension. Philosophy was left with some old cardboard boxes filled with the stuff science had no use for, morality, metaphysics and language, as well as some post-Romantic pop-psychology which coalesced into existentialism. That and a broken guitar and some CDs with cracked cases. From there, it was just some pyrotechnics and a little snake oil, and we got the three-ring circus of structuralism, post-structuralism, and post-modernism. These were like having the bad hangover without the pleasure of getting drunk first."

Now, a second love story. Vanikin, the lover of philosophy, was also the lover of a woman, Clara, who "was pretty rather than beautiful, a Raphael flower-maid rather than a Cimabue damsel or a fat-arsed Reubens roustabout." Clara, like Harry, is — or, rather, was — a philosopher: "We had a mutual love of Herodotus and Schopenhauer, cross disciplinary pollination which seemed naturally to lead to other activities undertaken by birds and bees the world over." The physical side of their love fails in reproduction, but even Harry's infertility is made into a humorous jab at the failures of the United Kingdom's modern welfare state: "Vanikin sperm seemed about as willing to work as contemporary British youth."

Harry's lady-love, Clara, is snatched out of his life in an instant by a pantechnicon truck — a giant furniture delivery vehicle — that hydroplaned on a wet road and then "batted Clara's funny little car into an oak tree and killed her... It rained at the funeral, and, for me, it would never stop raining."

After coaxing out this sorrow for the reader relatively late in the novel, the narration takes a dramatic turn, a turning of our Lazarus toward resurrection. Thus begins the third of the love stories embedded in the telling of Professor Vanikin's experience in the underworld from which he will emerge. It is the love of Estrella for her friend, the battered and morose savant professor who has lost two of his loves: Clara, and the teaching of philosophy.

Bringing Professor Vanikin back to life is a challenging project for Estrella, who becomes his amanuensis, agent, and teaching assistant. Wishing not to give too much away of the ending, I would just add that there then unfolds a surprising and deeply touching twist that is rife with irony. Europa House, a petri dish of UK social engineering pathology, is where Harry discovers the human and spiritual inspiration to step back into the world of philosophy and return to his love of teaching.

Vanikin in the Underworld is an admirable piece of writing: as literature, philosophy, and iconoclasm. For anyone who might doubt that in a single work, the parts of philosophy and fiction might not be greater than the whole, *Vanikin* will put that to rest.

CHAPTER ONE

Inappropriate Teaching Methods

I dreamed last night I was being measured up for my burial suit. The odd thing was that I was still alive. That's right. Some mincing little chaffinch with a tape-measure round his neck was feeling me up, chalking outlines on butcher paper, cocking his birdy head to one side while he looked at my scrawny seventy-year-old frame, and all to the end of making a suit to grace Harry Vanikin's coffin, his lying in state. He didn't say anything, but I knew. That's one of the things about dreams that sets them apart from waking life: However strange or other they might be, you always know what's going on.

I say I had the dream last night, but I meant when I was last asleep. The windows here are blacked out by big theatre curtains. It could be day or night. There used to be tiny, ragged holes in the fabric — wounds from a moth invasion — and the daylight would announce itself through these tiny spaces, making it look like a knackered old planetarium. That's what the ancient astronomers thought stars were, light getting in through a bloody great dome a few hundred miles above the earth. How do we know they were wrong? Everything else in the modern world is built on lies, why not the stars, too? Make it all up, fabricate, weave, and spin. I stuck black gaffer tape on the holes, and now, it's as black in here as a crow's heart.

I used to burn candles, but I set fire to one of the walls,

and the boy now refuses to buy me any more. So, I switch on the electric light, the 40-watt bulb suddenly spewing out its pale-yellow effusion. Not pale enough for Vanikin. I asked the boy if the shop did 20-watt bulbs, 10. Can you get a 1-watt bulb? Could you see by its light? Perhaps I should learn to feel my way around this haunted palace, like a blind man. Once, when the boy was sick, Estrella did my shopping and brought me back a light bulb that looked like it had been a prop in a Russian science fiction movie of the 1960s. Estrella, tall and gangling, with an anachronistic flapper's face tending to the lengthy. The bulb was sculpted glass tubing, and Estrella said it was energy efficient. Like all young people now, she is the conscience for an entire planet. When she had gone, I broke the monstrosity with a ball-peen hammer to see what was inside and waited for the boy to get well and buy me a proper bulb.

At the moment, the boy is well. He rarely gets ill, but he is on the right side of puberty, untroubled by the itches and drives that arrive when poisonous hormones leak into the childish glands. He is, however, prey to the natural maladies of the young. I don't know what time it is; watches and clocks simply sneer at you concerning your own mortality. When the boy comes, I know it is morning. He is a part of the overworld, and he has a mother to keep him on the temporal straight and narrow. His mother is called Manda. Not Amanda. Just Manda. I saw her once, peering in at my humble dwelling like a medieval courtesan gazing in wonder into a turf-cutter's hovel. She lives with the boy in one of the other rooms. The boy has a similarly mutated modern name, but to me, he is just the boy, a beacon of innocence in a world as rank as month-old cheese in a long-broken refrigerator.

The house has yet to come to life, so it must be early in the morning. The boy used to chatter away of his adventures in the overworld, giving away clues as to the season. I forbade him ever to speak of it again. I carry enough of the infection from outside, and I am here for the cure, to take the waters. Winter or summer, equinox or solstice; these climatic mood swings no longer concern me.

No. That's a lie too far. You will become used to my lies, my swingeing embellishments and outright deceptions, but let's not run before we can walk, or walk before we can crawl, or crawl before we have oozed from our mother's great tented bellies. Of course, I know the seasons even here, down here in the underworld. It is summer now. There is no need for the convection heater, and the caretaker of the building in which I live has turned off the central heating. The caretaker is a man called Craig McCerrow, and he is one of the most frightening of God's creations. God, or whoever runs this spiteful orb. But it is summer now.

Summer, too, when I first descended from the glare, down into the bowels, searching for no Eurydice but the truth, or at least a truth. 'Supposing truth to be a woman,' wrote Nietzsche, who slept with one woman in his life, who gave him syphilis, which drove him mad and left him in the Jena asylum for eleven years. Beware truth. Summer when I came here, seven summers ago, and in those seven years, I have left this room for a period in excess of twenty-four hours once and once only. Of which, more later.

Inappropriate teaching methods drove me here — or, led me here, the distinction being a part of the purpose of my visit — and I have to say that is pretty rich coming from the gauleiters of the overworld. I taught inappropriately? In a world where pinheaded advertising executives spend Third-World-economy-sized amounts selling children plastic and rubber shoes endorsed by multi-millionaire hoodlums who made their own fortunes braying about violent sex acts and ballistic weapons, my teaching methods were inappropriate? In a world in which banks deemed too big to fail are paid to survive by money taken from the pockets of toilet cleaners and nurses before awarding their incompetent executives yearly bonuses outstripping the amount those same cleaners and nurses would need to live for as long as a dozen Roman empires to earn, my teaching methods were inappropriate? In a world in which women can become men and men women on the state's ticket, children can view buggery at any hour of the day or night, screaming dervishes knife octogenarians as they queue for the bus, actors are asked about the world economy, simpering and large-breasted women lie about the weather to make themselves a fortune, shallow graves dot woodlands when men are done with their entertainments, and no one is allowed to use the word 'spastic' even though it comes from the ancient Greek 'spasmos,' which, meaning as it does 'to tremble violently', adequately describes the condition it used to stand for, and my teaching methods were inappropriate?

'Mr. Vanikin?'

Outside the door, the boy is here. I shuffle to the door and release the latch, tacky with age, and open the door an eye's width, checking that this is not that dreadful sprite Adam, with his abilities, his mimicry, and othernesses. It is not. It is the boy. I retreat back to the safety of my geriatric sofa, my large bald flannel dressing-gown's train following like a sick dog.

The boy is about twelve but already tall. Christ knows what there is in food nowadays, but it's not just the post-war boons I remember, iron and calcium and phosphates. Nowadays, the junk they shovel down must be crammed with alchemised plant food, kerosene, plutonium. The boy is tall but not independent of limb like Estrella. He already has co-ordination and grace, a larval godling. His mop of curly hair falls over one hazel eye. He would have gone down handsomely in the Athenian square, fawned over by a gaggle of Socrates' loquacious bum-chums.

Don't worry, little boys are not what the young people call 'my thing.' Christ alive, what do you do if you find out it *is* your thing? Lars, the middle-aged Danish laboratory worker who sometimes sits with me and brings me newspaper snippets from the world of men, like a paunchy Scandinavian Mercury, tells me there has been a spate of arrests of 'celebrities' over child abuse back in the days when men were all wearing Neanderthal sideburns and velvet jackets with landing-strip lapels. What actually happens on the day you discover that little girls — or little boys — *are* your thing? You are sitting on the tube train opposite a cherub. The swinging legs, the flash of tiny knicker cloth, the empathic pull in the sinews of the unruly member... Jesus, do you make straight for the nearest hospital, the nearest cop shop, or do you embrace your new vocation and head for darker infernal regions? Or are we, to use another phrase beloved of today's academic grubs and pupae, just 'ethnocentric' about all this? African tribes and their child brides. Nine-year-old Aisha shepherded into a tent to meet the patiently waiting Mohammed.

The boy has come into the room and is standing tapping at his ever-present mobile telephone, the portal to elsewhere beloved of all modern youth.

'What do you need today, Mr. Vanikin?'

'Um, the usual, really.'

I hand him my list, a pathetic inventory in a crabbed hand. Harry Vanikin's needs, strip-lit libations. The boy looks down at the meagre collection of items and pries loose the twenty-pound note carefully stapled to the torn strip of copier paper. He says,

'Craig says the water's got to go off today for two hours. Shall I fill the kettle right up?'

He's a good boy. If the child is father to the man then the world has a treat coming its undeserving way. The boy will not grow up to be Craig, crackling with malice, finding his way into a job with people, I'm certain, because people are his sport. The water is always having to go off, the lights go out, the heating fade to tepid, so that gangs of mythical 'workmen' can tinker and prise. The block is like some great sick mastodon tended by pygmy veterinarians.

The boy has gone, striding down to Ahmed's shop, and I am alone, or as alone as I can be. Vanikin in the underworld. Where were we? Ah, yes. Inappropriate teaching methods. I suppose it could have been worse. Socrates got the hemlock, Bruno, Wycliff, and Savonarola the stake and the fire, looking down and hoping the breeze was ministering to the flames. The university simply made no fuss and paid me my pension before laying me off. Estrella tells me my book is no longer to be found in the library reference system. My book. So much to tell.

Another day in my circle. I rip off a puckered square of kitchen roll and evacuate my nose into it before looking down to view the outcome, a Kandinsky miniature in grey, green, and red. My stomach, that aged coil of plumbing, is making small spiral noises, like tiny springs emerging from a captor mattress, and I must prepare porridge.

In the 'kitchen' — the square boarded off by prefabricated and hastily painted and wonky boards — I line up oats, salt, milk, a cup of water, and sugar on the ugly Formica surface. I turn the hob to three — hob, Anglo-Saxon word for the devil. Now, a circle of fire. Everything is present everywhere else; the human task is to sort it into piles that make sense.

I make porridge exactly the same way my father did, the big, bearded man who was as good to me as he knew how to be. Porridge must not be a swimming gruel, but neither must it be industrial adhesive. It should exist betwixt and between the two extremes, like we poor ape-angels.

As I carry the bowl back into the central space and the

retired sofa, I realise I must not have slept at all well.

CHAPTER TWO

The Fall of Mulciber

Just as every version of the underworld has its guardian or attendant devil, infernal factotum or dog of three heads, so, too, Europa House has Craig McCerrow. There he is now, shirtlessly grappling with some ancient lead fixture in the sweltering boiler room deep in the basement. His upper body is a patchwork quilt of tattoos, some professionally applied and some of more homemade provenance. They record past dalliances, the names of Craig's awful sociopathic children, tribal affiliations in the world of association football, nationalistic aspiration, and mythical creatures, zombie overlords, and full-breasted, broadsword-wielding vixens. Craig's mental life is correspondingly crammed and chaotic, but he is grateful for the job of resident caretaker at Europa House.

Indeed, the job was a godsend. Craig had had quite enough of his regular employment as doorman of various risk-laden speakeasies across the city. He had been stabbed and shanked, shivved and striped too many times to justify the money and drugs he received in payment for plying his precarious trade, and the caretaker's role allowed him to exercise power without the accompanying perils of the order of clientele to which he had become used. His biography presented here is a composite work, for which I must note the reportage of residents Lars, Declan, Ricky Rick, and Mrs. Podolski, who together form a sort of BBC World Service concerning the happenings at

Europa House.

I dread Craig. On the few occasions he had been inside my cubicle here at the House, I had cringed in the corner while he attended to trip switch or faulty tap, and he seemed exactly what he was, a dreadful man in a city of dreadful men. There is an order of being which seems to take place, to take its place, in a parallel dimension to that in which we, the weak and frail and fallible, live and breathe and have our being. To see Craig McCerrow, his sleeveless shirt showing enough of the hinterland of his squamously illustrated body to indicate his likely passage through life thus far, is to see a type of hell.

Now, he has simply turned off the water to the entire block to attend to some dysfunction in the ancient plumbing. Alerted by the boy, I have filled saucepans and the kettle and the old tin pail for my ablutions. Two hours was mentioned, but Craig keeps to no earthly temporal calibration. Once, he turned off the electricity for an afternoon but was persuaded by one of his appalling coterie of friends to go on a three-day drink-and-drug field exercise, and Europa House remained plunged in darkness for the duration.

As I accept that it is the morning, I must prepare for my day. I heat water in my kettle, testing the great orange gas container with the ball-peen hammer to see how much remains. We are all of us hooked up to these containers, and Craig replaces them for a stipendiary fee when they expire. There is no working gas supply system at Europa House, a fact which exercises the gangling Estrella. She, like most of her generation, is well versed on her rights, and claims that the contraptions which Craig has rigged up in each of our battery cells — the original house has been divided and divided again to provide more hutches for the inhabitants — contravene various Health and Safety commandments. I wouldn't know about that, although I do know that the last representative from the council to visit Europa House was so menaced by Craig that he had to take a month's sick leave from his place of work. That awful hobgoblin Bertie Spedding told me that. Bertie Spedding, the Mercury of bad news and sniffer of ill winds.

My water ready in the singing kettle, I fill the basin, select a flannel — a choice of two, royal blue and washing-machine grey — and begin to soap and valet the various cracks and orifices of my awful old body. 'The body,' writes Plato. 'A shadow which keeps us company.' I can't have a bath because the bath has a crack in it like lightning-split timber. It also has about a hundredweight of academic papers, newspapers, notepads dense with my scrawl, coverless books. Research, you see, for my next book, the follow up to my university-banned and universally unread debut. More later.

With my cleansed frame snugly inside my billowing dressing gown once more, I sit and read, transported to wherever today's book — the first of many — will take me. Reading is life to me, the phrases, ideas, concepts, new words and formulations all pouring into the old Vanikin head like wine into a cracked gourd. 'I would rather be a notepad for the sayings of great men,' writes the pugnacious Julius Caesar, 'than be a great man myself.' Some time later, I rest my book on the frayed elbow of the sofa's arm-rest as I hear the light tappity-tap on my door which announces the arrival of Lars and the news.

Lars is a bald and shiny domed Dane who was once a laboratory assistant before retirement drew him to the dubious environs of Europa House. He eschewed a return to the Norse land of his fathers on the grounds that it was now overrun by Mohammedans to an extent that not even the sleeping Holger Danske — the giant but currently comatose defender of the Danish people — could ever counter. He and I sit washed by my pale bulb, and Lars will tell me of affairs in the wider world, carefully précising the main currents of activity before expanding on one or two stories which have caught the attention of his enquiring Scandinavian mind, dutifully omitting to tell me the date.

Lars sits in my guest's chair, a sort of faux Regency throne with elegantly curved dark wood legs and the look of a creature with nocturnal habits all its own. Tufts of old horse-hair from a nag long dead protrude at intervals.

Lars speaks perfect English, retaining the slightly clipped tunefulness of his native land. His round-up of current affairs confirms the movements we all know to be taking place outside the ramparts of Europa House, as the world outside marches slowly but resolutely towards a second dark age, a sort of anti-Enlightenment. Money is still acting like an insane woman in the market square, all matted hair and flung excrement. Politicians still parade and speechify, like street vendors in the last minutes of Pompeii. The young still rule the streets while the old stay indoors, praying to gods who are themselves frightened. Motor cars still tear around culling the population, television still holds a nation in its mesmeric grip, and it has not rained for eleven days in a row. I make tea.

Lars and I sip at our hot brew as the amiable Dane begins a circumspect tour of what counts these days for news. News. The media. These old shades are part of the reason I fell from the heavenly ramparts of academia and landed here. I think of Milton's Mulciber in *Paradise Lost*, one of Satan's angels pushed — by Michael, if memory is a good and faithful servant — over heaven's battlements to fall to earth in a leafy forest, a descent which took a full day.

We are fallen, too. Crashing to earth where we sit huddled in a damp, loamy forest to be told tales by various spirits of the wood who do not have our well-being in mind. Inappropriate teaching methods. I tried to teach my students the truth; no one

told me the truth was no longer wanted. Think of Orwell —
lanky, pencil-moustachioed, public-school George — with his
fags and his TB. 'In a time of universal deceit, telling the truth
is a revolutionary act.' Vanikin the revolutionary, Vanikin in a
beret, bearded and chomping a cigar. I told them that Media
Studies, the degree for which so many of them clamoured like
ducklings at the water's edge, was a waste of time. Media studies
was what you did in your own time. Media studies was just
reading the papers and watching television. University
education should be more than a breakfast-time habit tenured.
Inappropriate teaching methods.

Lars is summing up the state of world affairs. But we all
know where the world is heading. It's heading here, to join
exiled Vanikin in the underworld. The world outside my retired
theatre curtains was a rickety pier full of whizzing circus rides
with the nuts and bolts all loosened and the lights off when I
last trod the boards. I tremble to think what it has become since
I groped my way below stairs, but I suspect that if I were to re-
emerge from my dank and Gyprocced chrysalis this very day, I
would not walk out into a second Renaissance.

It's consciousness, you see. Nietzsche called the brain our
last and least developed organ, and he was right — poor, mad,
syphilitic, old Friedrich. Giving consciousness to *homo sapiens*
was like giving the Large Hadron Collider — and there, Lars
did hold my attention — to a saloon bar full of association
football aficionados. There *was* the Renaissance, of course, but
it was hardly general issue. A Milanese peasant born the day Fra
Angelico was born and breathing his final rasping breath — a
rare octogenarian — the day Uccello passed away would, in all
probability, have lived his entire span without setting eyes on a
framed painting. A frame was what you grew your turnips in.
The Renaissance, the Enlightenment, modernism; these were
mostly things that happened to other folk, the folk on the hill.

The majority of the world's population went on much as before while Michelangelo was creating his wonders, dirt under the nails and trying not to get killed by their neighbours. My tea is cold, and Lars has finished his report.

I bid Lars a fond farewell in his native Danish. *Farvel.* It more or less exhausts my knowledge of that jolly-sounding language, and sounds to me like a minor character from a Dickens novel. Little Farvel. Dickens, with his mad hair and social conscience.

I feel vaguely unclean after being sprayed with the ordure of the outside world, and I head for my bathtub. I retrieve something soothing and recline on the buggered sofa, wondering who the house will throw at me next.

Europa House was built at the start of the 1960s, and so has no exterior charm and resembles a hybrid of an East German tax office and a giant lock-up by a ring road. As mentioned, the original spacious apartments have been cordoned and sub-divided and partitioned to produce the current human hen-house, and I am merely one lonely occupant among many. A surprising proportion of the inhabitants are, by any reasonable usage of the phrase, clinically insane — I am one — but there are gems amid the chaos. Part sanctuary for the disenfranchised, part asylum, part dormitory, part ghost train, Europa House has been my abode these seven years since my public disgrace and defenestration. After the fall, this is my pandemonium.

No one came to see me as I cleared my office at the university. To associate with Vanikin was to be on McCarthy's blacklist, in the FBI's little black book, marked down for a Leninist show trial. I had become toxic, a pariah or *pharmakos* or scapegoat. And so, for seven years, I have wandered in the desert of myself, apart from the ways of men…

A small drum-roll at my hollow door. The boy has returned

with my provisions. I trust him with my pension, giving him a small stipendiary consideration, of which I suspect Manda would not approve. All modern mothers believe that all elderly men are sexual predators, with their offspring squarely in the crosshairs. The danger, however, lurks elsewhere. Mentally and intellectually, the peril starts when teacher arrives with her curriculum of anti-life skills. Outside the school gates, meanwhile, the drug dealers lurk.

The boy, as always, leaves two gossamer-thin carrier bags outside my warped front door, and I retrieve them like a laboratory rat snatching at a food pellet.

Tinned fruit, tinned meat, cordial, tea, milk, biscuits, porridge oats. Ahmed's prices are reasonable, and I have purchased enough to keep a sub-Saharan family for most of a week. I have modest requirements; such is the life of the fallen angel, the outcast scowling back at the city of the sun, the *civitas solis*.

CHAPTER THREE

Estrella and the Arriviste

Oh, I was good. Standing room only when Prof. Vanikin gave a lecture, scuffles at the door of a room full to bulging. The subject matter didn't, as it were, matter; it was me they were coming to see. Gloomily, I reflect that they come still to my current hut in the forest, tiny pilgrimages in this battery-farm crazy house, but more of that anon. My seminars, too, over-subscribed and crawling with student life. I taught them about Spinoza and Wittgenstein, Descartes and Heidegger, Hume and Berkeley. I tried to draw it out of them, the philosophical urge, the itch to enquire, to ask of the universe: And you are? I wanted to make them see what they already knew, like the angles lurking unseen deep within the soul of Meno's slave boy, the shy youngster Socrates questions about geometry, who has all the answers without knowing it. Then, the strange thing happened.

Lunch is a modest affair: corned beef and a puffy white roll liberally smeared in a butter substitute of the yellow colour found in a child's paint-box, followed by tinned pineapple rings, stacked neatly in their alloy cylinder on top of one another like tiny vinyl records, swimming in a sweet syrup flecked with pulp. Is it a coincidence that the rise of the tin coincided with the onset of nuclear armaments? How could you prepare for Armageddon and a barren nuclear winter with fresh food? The atom bomb versus the tin. Man sets up another binary, another conflict to set alongside the others. To drink, I favour milk.

A sudden jolt back to childhood. I arrive like a B-movie time-traveller outside my primary school. The stout little milk bottles, with their silver foil tops, sitting in metal crates on a very cold winter day. The temperature has frozen the water all milk must contain, the foil tops have risen from the bottles perhaps three quarters of an inch, a column of frozen white pushing upwards, expanding to the tune of a coefficient. In summer, the milkman would set an empty crate on top of the full one he left at some tiny hour, the second crate to keep off the blue tits, who would peck through the foil and drink at the creamy upper deck of the milk. Myself, as milk monitor, stabbing the tit-protected foil with a small pair of scissors, trying to do it as fast as possible. The plastic beakers with their different colours — some slightly chewed at the lip — the white moustaches on the upper lips of the small children around me as they tipped their glasses inexpertly...

Sometimes, I suffer from the cascade of memory. The past begins as a trickle, a laughing brook, but soon becomes a flash-flood, a torrent of images, *Remembrance of Things Past* re-written as an eyewitness account of a medieval siege. I finish my milk. There is a light tap at the door. I have come to learn the distinctive morse of the inmates here, the boy's urbane and rhythmic four beat, the flurried snare roll of Mrs. Podolski, Lars' dom-da-DOM-dom syncopation, the single primeval clump of Craig's ham-like fist. This fairy trill can only be Estrella, and so it is.

At a little under six feet, Estrella is about six inches taller than me. She is all angles and bony sharpness. Even by her own high standards, today, she is agitated, flicking at her hair, a funfair of neurotic tics and feints. I wordlessly prepare the tea she likes, one of those unholy mixtures of woodland weeds sold to a gullible public as 'herbal teas'. I serve this potion to a sitting and clearly troubled Estrella. I have many teas, coffees, and infusions. My visitors have varied tastes, and visit they do. Due to some vast cosmic gag, some metaphysical comedy sketch, I have taken up the role of guru to the denizens of Europa House. Arbitrator, father confessor, non-directional psychotherapist, I've become a sort of old man of the mountain in a frayed dressing gown. Now Estrella shares her burden.

It would seem that we have an arriviste in our midst, a new tenant, a stranger in a strange land. I wonder when his supplication to my hutch will begin. Estrella voices her fears and doubts.

'I'm just not sure about him, Harry. He had nothing with him when he moved in.'

'And he is in Mr. Carter's old flat, you say?'

'Yes.'

'Well, Estrella, I believe Mrs. Glasspool rents that flat furnished.'

'But he had no clothes or books. No saucepans. He didn't have any *bathroom* things.'

Perhaps, Estrella, I want to say, he is uncluttered by the endless inventory of the modern. Maybe he eschews the ranks and files of supermarket detritus. Perhaps he's a Buddhist, with a mat and a bowl. Estrella, though, I can see, wants him to be a serial killer, an MI5 intelligence agent, a fugitive from the law, a racist. Estrella, in the plight of her boredom and frustration at her lack of meaningful purpose, wants her own little Northanger Abbey, brimming with Gothic mystery.

'I don't like him. He didn't say hello.'

'Some men are shy with women, Estrella.'

'Are they?'

Yes, they are. And some aren't. The last time I was outside the box of my existence, I was constantly appalled at the leering approaches, the satyromaniacal lunges, that the men of this once fair kingdom made at the womenfolk. And the women didn't seem to mind. No policemen were called, no shrieks of outrage rent the air. It's not that I'm getting old — although I am — but that the world is ageing faster than I am, outpacing an old man in its rush to a dribbling, incontinent dotage where everything will be okay to do and say and everyone will go ahead and do and say it, all the time and to everyone.

'Perhaps you should ask the letting agency.'

'They'll just think I'm mad again.'

That sentence is the graven motto arching over the entrance to the prison of Estrella's life. She has, indeed, been incarcerated under section 28 of the 1983 Mental Health Act — this makes us colleagues, of which, more later — a borderline schizophrenic whose condition used to be controlled by between 50 and 100ml of Chlorpromazine a day. That is a very strong dosage of a very strong drug. She is vastly improved, it should be noted. Estrella has finished her tea and declines the offer of more.

'No, thanks, Harry. I have to go and read to Molly Schumpeter.'

And sad Estrella takes her leave. I am not a young man, and so, I am untroubled by imaginings concerning Estrella, what it might be like to stand suddenly before her, tease a wisp of her hair from over one eye, and push back the dull grey shoulders of her Puritanical cardigan. I'd need a step-ladder, in any case. But I wonder idly if she has romantic attachments, whether she forgets her condition and gives herself up to caresses, to little nibbles and exhalations.

Estrella is aware of her own condition. I would call it auto-gnostic, if anyone were to ask me my opinion, which they haven't, although there is a chapter on it in The Banned Book, to which we will return. We've talked about it, she and I. She hears voices, that illusion so favoured by the inner imps of schizophrenia. Curiously, though, Estrella's small symposium of advisers — 'there's more than one; I've got names for them all' — do not go down the well-beaten path of exhortations to suicide, the endless nihilistic commentary that accompanies most sufferers from that curious condition. In fact, they sound an affable lot, always chit-chatting of this and that, passing the time of day like middle-aged women in a supermarket queue.

So, the arriviste. He has moved into the flat a floor down from myself, recently vacated by Mr. Carter, a retired bus driver who inherited money from a, presumably long-lost, uncle and moved to Malta. Although I may have given the impression that I held sway over Europa House — Prospero in his formica and linoleum cave — not everyone visited, and Mr. Carter never did; he kept himself very much to himself, a normal guy, as interviewed neighbours like to say about the latest urban slayer or pervert or jihadi.

The day must be reaching maturity. I read and snooze, snooze and read. I dine royally on game soup — it has a painting of a stag on the front of the tin — and fruit-pie filling in syrup. Thinking of Europa House's new tenant, my mind returns unprompted to my own arrival at my current station. My sister took care of my relocation from the hospital. We'll come to the hospital.

On my first day here, I met Craig, Estrella, and the boy, as well as Pilkington, the writer who lives below me and who I can hear singing and peeing and sobbing as he tries to wring from himself the book that will end all the questioning once and for all time.

They are among the dramatis personae of Europa House, and you will meet them all. All human life may not be here, but I feel a pollster would accept the place as a representative sample of what it is to be human in Great Britain and not to have very much money.

Actually, in financial terms, I am a Tuscan duke in a hillside villa watching the peasants tend their wretched vines in comparison with my colleagues here at the House. I worked in the public sector, you see, on one of those contracts that promised — and supplied — a very great deal of money once you finished your tenure in the dark Satanic mill of the British education system, although they flayed my pension as punishment for my transgressions.

But I have money, in the context of Europa House. For this is benefit land, quite literally the land of the free, with a few notable exceptions. Please don't take me for a snob; a man cannot look down on a man who looks him straight in the eye. I forget who wrote that. Until such time as I remember, I'm claiming it for my own. Marek, the clever little Steerpike from Gdansk who pops in to drink his strong Polish lager and smoke extremely pungent cigarettes, says that everyone can think of clever things, but not everyone can say them. When he told me that, little did he suspect that he would cost me much sleep and even more reading time.

Enough of money. Lars tells me the world is running out of the stuff. Not only that, the stuff they are running out of didn't exist in any meaningful sense of the word before they started running out of it. The whole credit system that supports the West like the turtle the ancients thought supported the (flat) earth was ably described to me by Lars. It sounded as likely to succeed as building a card house using digestive biscuits. But my money arrives, courtesy of the university and transferred to me in doses by my sister, with a regularity I find a little shocking in this day and age. But you have yet to meet my sister, who I suspect is not mere flesh and blood, but the next generation of AI.

It is night-time now. I get used to the rhythms of the house, the entrances and exits, the televisions and radios and fights. I read — or, I try — but I lose concentration. I think about the new arrival. How will he change the psychic machinery of the House? If he is single, there are unattached women here, including Estrella. Perhaps his brusqueness will unlock some gnawing desire deep in Estrella's modest breast. How will he deal with the voices, though? Their pillow talk would be like a cheese-and-wine party.

Will he visit me? It surprises and amuses me that I have now looked at newcomers to Europa House as conscripts or askers of directions on a busy street.

This building is a hive, a machine, a puzzle, and a boardgame all at the same time. It is this kind of thinking, I am inclined to believe, that got me into trouble in the first place. Systems. Interconnections. I left the university with a sort of politically incorrect honourable discharge. Then, I went mad.

CHAPTER FOUR

In the TV Room

I watched an awful lot of television while I was in the hospital. The TV room was the nerve-centre of the operation, a spacious, ill-painted mausoleum where those of us who still had some connection with the world — at least a version of it — would sit and stare at the television set as though it were a pagan idol and we the primitive islanders paying obeisance to the deity.

Television is more of an education concerning the modern world than any course taught by my trendy former colleagues in the Sociology department could ever bequeath to its students. What arch time-wasters these people are, their own time and the far more valuable time of their students. Media Studies. Non-white Studies. Lesbian, Gay, Bisexual and Transgender Studies. Colonial Studies. Queer Studies. Beware any course in further education which has the word *studies* appended to it because studying is one of many standard academic procedures in which you will not be taking part. These hobbyist grudge farms have nothing to surprise you, no card up their respective sleeves, when you set them next to the television.

The alchemists would have swooned if their attempts to transmute lead into gold had suddenly granted them their goal, in a puff of wizard's smoke. They would have been even more open-mouthed at the television, although, of course, in the case of the telly — the 'idiot box,' as my mother used to refer to it — and its reduction of the wonders of the world, this would have been the equivalent of turning gold into lead, but you take my point.

Daytime television was an Elysian field of apparently attainable aspiration. Chefs, gardeners, antiques dealers, interior designers, more chefs. It is as though they are reading Biblical lessons from a strange new translation, lessons from a televisual pulpit. Television is, without question, the single most deleterious, dangerous, addictive, malignant medium currently in existence. I was fascinated.

The advertisements alone cast a fierce glamour over me. Some adverts used sensational specimens of the human race, cartoonishly beautiful gods and goddesses, a Greek pantheon behind their steamed and sliding plastic shower doors, slathering themselves with brightly coloured gel as the power-shower cascaded them with crystal water. Perfect couples with perfect teeth and perfect children would set off in gleaming motor-cars to places even more perfect than those they were leaving. And then, in an almost bucolic gesture, other offerings would feature very, very ordinary people — or, at the very least, the median of a very, very normal person, as triangulated by the armies of image-makers who presumably make the whole world of advertising run.

Perfume or cologne would require two beings just now having filtered down from the heavens. A motor-car had need of two attractive but, broadly speaking, efficient spouses. A casino might also need attractive figureheads, but they would be harder faced than the car duo, and far more sluttish. The catalogue of power tools needed just one man, the man who looks exactly like the man standing next to you at the pub bar. I began to understand. Life, I mean, not advertising.

More news on the arriviste. Declan drops by with a half-bottle of god-awful Scotch and some Temazepam. I have a nip of the former in a tooth-glass, foregoing the latter, and topped it right up with tap water. I'm not a great drinker. I read somewhere that Churchill's reputation as being permanently semi-sozzled was — like so much of modern life — largely myth. He would certainly start drinking early, but he drank one Scotch and water — brimful, like mine — and sipped at it all morning. Christ — and the War Cabinet and Clemmie — alone knows what debauches lunch and dinner saw, but we beat the Hun. Declan.

Declan tells me that our new recruit is Caucasian and solidly built, unfriendly, and taciturn. 'Hard, stockish, and full of rage,' as Shakespeare — not Declan — put it. One of the Henrys? Declan is already of the opinion that the new man — he remains nameless — and Craig should have a fight. I ask him why.

'To see, loik, who wins.'

'You've begged the question.'

'Have I, fock?'

'What would happen to the winner?'

'What winner?'

Declan often gives the impression that his short-term memory operates in nano-seconds rather than more usual units of time.

'The winner of the fight between Craig and the new man.'

Declan was already starting to succumb to the various drugs, both prescription and otherwise, he always seemed to have about him, or actually inside him. Sometimes, he would fall asleep, and I would watch, fascinated and guilty, as he lolled and spoke in tongues. Was that all it was, divine revelation? Did Joseph, Moses, and Mohammed just take a lot of Temazepam? Declan fights back, and replies.

'The winner would have supremacy, loik. Of the building.'

'Do you think Europa House is like that? Like the jungle?'

'Course it is. And I'm a cheeky focking monkey, and you're a wise old…lion. Or a bear. Anyway, thanks for the tea, Mr V.'

Declan has had no tea, just slugs of whiskey, but I acknowledge his thanks, and off he goes — surprisingly sprightly for a young man habitually embalmed in cheap Scotch and tax-funded barbiturates — to his next chaotic rendezvous.

I realised early what it was I liked about Declan. He never has anything to do because he never has to do anything. Ever, at all. He lives on benefits and the proceeds of drug-dealing. He drinks and takes drugs all the live-long day, and so, a conversation with him is not time-urgent, like that of some in the sector of society which still works for a living.

Honestly, I don't believe that it marks out a man politically to say that I find it absolutely extraordinary — almost beyond conception — that Declan can live in the style to which he has long been accustomed without those who brass up for his extended leisure time in The Leather Pig spontaneously marching to Westminster, home of the great British mother of all parliaments, with pitch-soaked and flaming brands in their hands. I don't, honestly. The point, I suppose, is whether or not you approve of it, and I have no strong feelings either way.

Could I live like Declan? Perhaps I should try. But I would always have the safety net of money; Declan walks the trapeze wire with no such safeguard. He has never borrowed money from me, nor have I offered it. And yet, he is a hunter-gatherer by any other name. I suppose when a young man of today's ilk calls you a wise old lion — or, as an alternative, a bear — you will have a soft spot for him.

Sometimes, Declan, during his slobbering periods of demonic possession in my guest chair, will utter the name Eileen. Is this some past paramour from the Emerald Isle, some Colleen waiting for his return in a pub in County Whatever?

His mother? His parole officer? Other people's lives.

There was a young man at the hospital, an auxiliary nurse working during his summer between school and university. He still called it 'university' then, of course, and not 'uni,' as the young of today call that venerable institution. Soon, 'university' will seem as archaic a word as 'manufactory.'

His name was Alex, and he was going to study mechanical engineering. I asked him one day what he would like to build, and he told me a fascinating story.

It appears that the father of one of Alex's friends had been to India on business. His was a mining concern, and he was shown a Lister diesel engine used to pump the inevitable monsoon water from a shaft. The wonderful thing was that the engine had been running continuously for twenty-five years, with running repairs carried out while reducing the engine's rev count down to about ten per second. One day, said Alex brightly, I want to build machines that never break down, that you can fix without turning them off, that fix themselves.

Machines that fix themselves. I suppose that's what we are. But we are the only animal who must fix himself — sorry, feminists and post-feminists and all points West. I'm always using male pronouns. Sign of age combined with a sense that language is still free to those who have disappeared underground — those like me — mentally as well as physically. Or at least keep the thing running, effecting minor repairs as time allows, and with the revs down...

This, I became convinced, was why I had come to the hospital; this was my low-revving period, after which I would emerge like a butterfly and write the book for which philosophy, in all her finery, had been waiting so long. Appalling syntax, I know, but I'm excited just thinking back to the bright ward with its deep maternal curves and peppermint walls. I was waiting for the message from above. My sister

Nadia visited often, gliding in like a sinister Queen of Sheba, with Yevgeny, her dreadful son, my nephew. Alas, no message.

Declan's arrival and departure give me no clues as to the time of day or night it might be. Declan keeps irregular hours, in keeping with his calling, and it could equally easily have been four in the morning or four in the afternoon. Something tells me, though, that it is daytime. Some deep, atavistic, reptilian twitch speaks to me of the day.

Philosophy. We'll come to that. I remember overhearing — during my last sane days in the overworld — a businessman telling a pub colleague about *his* philosophy. It seemed to have as its main aim the extinction of the entirety of mankind, along with more or less all other non-viral and non-microbial life, in exchange for the human right to watch the television channel of your choice. Perhaps, I thought, I'm paying too much attention to my students. Perhaps I've come over all Left-wing.

No. I must eat. Estrella has told me all about the wonders of nutrition. Nutrition and all its works. 'What can I know?' asked Immanuel Kant. 'What can I eat?' asks the post-modern generation. What, indeed. Now that the human race no longer has to spend its entire waking time foraging for sufficient food to give it the required energy to stay alive all day in order to keep foraging for sufficient food to give it the required... Food.

I peruse my war rations. A little while ago, I recalled a programme from the hospital in which a chef cooked various dishes enjoyed, so he claimed, by the world's many and various historical peasantry. I was much taken by rice and beans. It had an aroma of delta blues and something imperceptibly South American about it, and perhaps it spoke to my inner raffish gaucho, I suppose. It also, sadly, made me fart like some hideous ancient Gatling-gun, and I was genuinely frightened in the morning, not daring to touch anything electrical — fear of the spark! — until I had fully ventilated my living quarters. The smell of our own farts. Odour of decay. The perfume of death. Charnel by Chanel. I must rest.

I do more than rest, I snooze. I am about to get my visa stamped at the gates of the Land of Nod when there is a spidery scraping at the door, that balsa wood rice-biscuit protecting me from the horrors of the overworld. I know instinctively who is without. It is Magda. I feel a sense of comfort mingle inexpertly with a sense of dread.

CHAPTER FIVE

Magda and the Measuring Man

Magda, with her witchy ways, her premonitions and visions, a Jacobean aura about her no Enlightenment could ever scrub off. Cassandra with a dustpan and brush, a misplaced Serb from the gypsy enclaves of that frayed country, Magda's role at Europa House is both clear and unclear. She cleans, that much is transparent, as clear as any grime-besmirched surface she cares to touch eventually becomes. She is a first-rate cleaner. Dirt obeys her, does her bidding, and leaves the premises, the county, the country. It may leave the planet, for all I know, its race run on earth and in search of other worlds to make dirty. But alongside the Magda who marches through Europa House like Delacroix's *Liberty Leading the People* — with a Hoover instead of a flag and without the bared breasts — another Magda moves silently in a parallel dimension, ghosting alongside like a shadow in storm light. This is no product of Vanikin's reclusive imagination. Craig is frightened of Magda, which in itself speaks eloquently of power, of a deep well of force and ley. Magda of the old ways.

She is not a gypsy in our ridiculous modern sense, of course, not some copper-stripping Mick tinker with LOVE and HATE tattooed across her fat pocked knuckles, and a house with a pool outside County Claire courtesy of the mainland taxpayer. Lars hints ominously, aided and abetted by one or other of the fat-headed newspapers, that half the English countryside is now seasonally invaded by these insurgent roustabouts, and there are regular stand-offs between the marauders and the toothless ranks of the police force. Magda is not of those. But neither is she a silk-turbaned pier mystic, glass globe and mist. No wicked pack of cards.

Magda cleans. She is the cleaner of Europa House, Our Lady of the Mops. And there is much to clean here, much in the way of filth even before we come to Vanikin's dirty old soul. My dressing gown shuffles to the door with me inside, and Magda's presence fills what there is of my room. She surveys my kingdom, and she finds it wanting.

'Oh, Mr. Vanikin. You have spilled coffee.'

'Yes, ah.'

This is another consequence of Magda's presence. Vanikin the wordsmith, the eloquent pedagogue, lecturer *non pareil*, writer of barely-read-yet-banned books, is reduced to little stutterances in the presence of Magda, black-clad naiad of the corridors and upward-facing surfaces. 'That whereof we cannot speak,' said the skinny neurotic queer Wittgenstein, 'we must remain silent.' He never met Magda, who makes it impossible for Vanikin the philosopher to say anything coherent about anything, whether we can speak thereof or not. Thus, I cannot offer her a coffee by anything more than deaf-mute gestures, coffee which she declines. Perhaps she limits herself to one cup a day of something prepared using *Macbeth* as a cookbook and not as it was intended.

As Magda sponges the sticky ichor of Vanikin's dysphasia, she says,

'There is new man. In Mrs. Glasspool's flat.'

'Yes, um.'

'I expect Estrella already tell you.'

Do you see? Even Vanikin's brainwaves do not escape Magda's unnatural antennae. She detects the psychic morse code of Europa House, translates and retains. I have an idea of the group psychology of Europa House, but Magda feels its flow in an almost artistic way. I pass my hand over my brow more as a gesture, a box-ticking exercise, than from any need to do so. Magda continues her astral observations.

'Estrella would know. She is fascinated with new man. As with all men. Well, you have been very good boy. Not much to do. Everything else hunky and dory, Mr. Vanikin?'

That dreadful Puck Adam teaches Magda these awful phrases, which she adapts like a mistress seamstress using an old lace rag as a hem and making good. Of that, I'm sure. I expostulate.

'Yes, um.'

And Magda vanishes behind the smoke of her mystery. How curious to hear my name spoken in the accents of the east, as my grandfather, a Russian émigré who once met Bukharin and stood in the streets as a boy watching Nadia Stalin's funeral — Nadia is a name which will recur, as it is my sister's name, and I always wonder... — would have heard it when he first had it changed and tried it out on a stern-eyed family elder. *Vennerkin*. It sounds like some unfinished novel by a friend of Gogol's. The Russian novel hasn't been written that could contain my family. I slump back in my pummelled — not by me — sofa, the dressing-gown quilting its slopes like dirty snow beneath a dim Siberian sun.

My grandfather, Yevgeny Pavlovich, arrived in the land of hope and glory in 1944 with, so he believed, the furies of the October Revolution snapping and snarling at his threadbare heels. The man on the SS Moravia whom my granddad fully believed was going to poison him, however, turned out not to be a Bolshevik hunter seeking to spear his Menshevik — as my grandfather was — but a shoemaker from Archangel who harboured the same paranoid qualms concerning Yevgeny Pavlovich, believing him to be carrying some species of blow-dart, poison-tipped umbrella, or vial of cyanide for the dinner table. They became firm friends, and laughed about the confusion throughout their long lives in England. Russians can laugh about the good side of bad things.

As surely as though Magda had summoned her shade merely by mentioning her name, by some powerful hex operating here in the underworld, Estrella arrives on a magic carpet of tics and squints and fidgeting. She has news of import from another circle of Europa House. Wordlessly, I begin to prepare a cup of non-tea, of homoeopathically altered hot water, and Estrella sits and fans herself with the stretched sleeve-end of her Virginia Woolf cardigan.

'Harry. This new man. I've seen him talking to Craig.'

'Introducing himself, I expect.'

'Craig never does that. Never.'

'No, but the new chap won't know that.'

Estrella is alive to the slightest behavioural nuance here at Europa House. From her frantic reports, I build a picture of a web of neuroses, and not just hers. She is simply the Greek chorus of this tragi-comedy, Europa House the stage for her complex succession of strophe and antistrophe. She talks on, staring straight ahead as though she sees some hobgoblin jeering in the corner of the room. Estrella says,

'And he's measuring.'

'He's measuring?'

It always repays one's time to confirm precisely what Estrella has said, as, in fact, it does with most of the cast of Europa House. The residents here are often not very far from automatic speech, as though they were channelling a lost and troubled spirit or gabbling in tongues in some Louisiana serpent church.

'He's measuring. The width of the corridors. The height of the doors. The size of the lift.'

'I expect he's from the council.'

'We don't have councils, Harry. We have local authorities now. No. He's up to something.'

Estrella, I want to cry out, my poor lanky booby, we're *all* up to something. That's what life is. Getting up to our old tricks. She finishes her nettle-and-twig infusion — or whatever I have randomly selected today. She rises like leaves being blown upwards by one of those contraptions park-keepers use, a reversed vacuum cleaner. She says,

'I'm going to talk to Adam.'

You may as well, I think, talk to the Cretan liar himself, if it's the truth you're after. But Estrella is gone, leaving behind a slight after-smell of peppermint and sweat. The room settles. So, too, Vanikin's thoughts. *Settle thy thoughts, Faustus, and begin...*

Vanikin is alone again, here, in the place he has chosen to escape to. Heidegger in the Black Forest, Byron at Missolonghi, Orwell on Jura, Nietzsche in Sils-Maria, Vanikin in Europa House. And escape? Hardly. No desert-bound stylite ever had a social life as vibrant and overfull as mine. For mine is the cottage door the path to which is beaten flat by the forest-dwellers of the welfare state. Vanikin the mad old hermit, wood-gatherer, the object of the queried gaze of Wenceslaus, recluse and rumoured author. Ah, yes. Yes. The fucking *book*.

The Decadent Turn. There, I've written it down. A book now on the *index prohibitorum*, unreadable by the dictates of laws which are no less real for being hidden, currently unavailable via major outlets, as the internet reliably informed Estrella and then me, in short order. Perhaps, in centuries to come, antiquarian adventurers might seek a copy in some Moroccan *souk*, in Lovecraft's Miskatonic Library, in the same dusty bookseller's where Nietzsche found, by chance, a copy of Schopenhauer's *The World as Will and Idea*. 'And it came about that he read, in a certain book…'

Pah! This has nothing to do with my book. This is the curse of the genius *manqué* — always to believe that the smallest pebble thrown into the mill-pond of everyday affairs will mount into a tsunami of self-relevance. The hospital. The TV room. The fights over the remote control, over which programme with which to blend our brains into smoothies. *You must learn to share, Harry. It's not all to do with you…*

I snooze. I dream — or, I think I do. The butterfly of Lao Tzu, dreaming he is a man dreaming he is a butterfly dreaming he is Descartes, unsure of whether he is dreaming. I snooze on. Measuring, measuring. Who is this snake in the grass, with his tape measure and his lack of jocularity, befriending Craig without offering narcotics or vats of cheap booze, the currency in which Craig — and many here in our urban Hades — deal? Estrella, the boy, Lars, the Measuring Man; all cavort in Vanikin's oneiric version of *La Ronde*…

And I awake to silence and darkness and the great dark space of the underworld, my lonely cell. Socrates, it was, in the *Phaedo*, facing death with what would become Stoicism, looking forward to the hemlock to speed him on his way to the underworld, there to meet with Homer and the greats. No welcoming committee for Vanikin, I suspect, and no hemlock, either. Along with his sister, a social worker and a nurse dropped him off at Europa House, special delivery from the asylum via Nadia's sternly organised apartments. Forms were signed and countersigned, but not by me, mad as the mist and snow as I still was at the time, despite my web of conceit spun at the hospital. Of *course*, I am still mad, you dolts, I thought. If I'm not, what on God's green earth does that make you?

The light summer rain fell on us all as they bundled me out of the taxi and into the underworld. I had to agree to being discharged from the address to which I was discharged and made a ward, and I would only be discharged in order to be rowed across the Styx to Europa House. The company acquiesced. The nurse, with a port-wine stain on her throat the exact shape of Belgium. The social worker, with dreadlocks like hempen hawsers at a boatyard and a gold tooth glinting like a pharaoh's casket. And the other one, the other Vanikin — née Vanikin. The architect of my down-going, a suburban Medea, my sister.

CHAPTER SIX

Preparations for a Royal Visit

Nadia Vanikin is a year older than me, an elder sister whose value to her errant brother has oscillated during my time on earth. On the occasion of my descent into the underworld, she was, I suppose, my Charon, rowing bonkers Vanikin across the Styx and into Europa House. She took care of me with an accountant's precision, and I don't *think* she is angling for my poor estate. I once suggested we swap musical ideas for our funerals, whoever snuffed it first getting to have the other's choice of despised tunes accompany them to the flames. She told me I was a morbid old sod. I have noticed that she likes English swear words, undoubtedly her idea of cultural assimilation. Nadia, then. Nadia, the female of the species Vanikin.

Retired now, Nadia was more or less retired throughout her career, having chosen an academic and professional route which she selected on the simple principle that it would make her a decent amount of money as well as intruding on her life as little as possible. Please do not misunderstand Vanikin. He knows fine well, as Declan would phrase it, the debt of gratitude he owes his stern and upright sibling. But she is a lair spider, and of that, all must beware.

There are those little spiders that charge about apparently webless, presumably eating on the go. Most spiders toil and weave, producing a deadly home, a deceptive piece of beautiful and welcoming architecture. But my sister is a lair spider, a spider who seeks a nook in which to live, and into which to entice others…

After training as a clinical psychologist, she became tired of helping people and went into management consultancy, a field of human endeavor on which she left her sword-slashed mark. She told me that firing someone is better for them than all the hours of therapy they could afford. Her lair is securely spun, and it is a web of the mind.

Of course, given the imp of the perverse that drives my sister through the psychological labyrinth of her own creation which doubles as her life, she has a child — more of a man-child — now in his mid-forties, and he is one of god's little spies, one of those far-from-idiotic *savants* who can dissect ideas. Talking to him makes me feel I am talking to a being from another galactic race, another mental dimension. Nadia and Yevgeny, refugees from some tribal pantheon of gods — or devils — somewhere.

Well, the boy tells me that it is the appointed day for a visit from our beloved spider. The boy is also my social equerry. She even *called* him, if you will. I use no mobile telephone, thank you all very much. I will not join the uniformed hordes staring into their goon-screens as though there were some great wisdom there. But, somehow, technology intrudes into Vanikin's life like an uninvited guest who nonetheless can help, if only by proxy. The witch of Prague and her demonic helper are descending to the underworld, there Vanikin for to seek.

We got on tolerably well as children. Nadia was always fascinated by other people, as though they were some quirky gimmick or thoughtful entertainment laid on by kind adults for a curious girl, like a full-size toy theatre. She told us once, at dinner and at the age of twelve, that, although we were pleasant enough people individually, we were utterly unfit to be a family.

Or words to the effect. And they did have an effect.

Nadia was always shunned by my father and mother. They indulged me, and what irritated them most, I believe still, was that Nadia's response to this clear sibling favouritism was not irritation, bitterness, or petulance but was as though yet another psychological drama had been put on, play-like, for her benefit and instruction. Life for Nadia was a great schoolroom in which, even as a student, she taught.

When she had Yevgeny, she asked me to be godfather, and I told her that a non-believer — never an atheist; none of that sugary brew for Vanikin — officiating over such a ceremony may adversely hinder any progress of the boy's soul through life. I was making a perfectly reasonable observation, which are often a casually tossed gauntlet to women, to the effect that if Nadia felt the spirit within sufficiently to desire a confirmation, then she would have to take the free picnic hamper that came with the ritual, the one that contained all the metaphysics.

She looked at me as though I was smeared with excrement, and she found another to pledge his soul for this ungodly child. As I have confided, Yevgeny has grown up to be a stealer of souls, a fearful town-crier who inflicts on you whatever he is reading at the time, be it mediaeval Latin poetry, Frege, Luther, Aleister Crowley, or all of those, confected into an awful dessert, to be eaten only when all hope has departed.

Estrella wafts at the door, and I let her in, with her cargo of neuroses and trousseau of tics and fidgets. I will indulge her then send her packing by mentioning my sister, who Estrella views, not altogether inaccurately, as a hybrid of Lucretia Borgia and Cruella de Ville. Estrella sits, then stands, then sits again and crosses and uncrosses her legs once and then again for form's sake. She says,

'Your sister is coming.'

'Yes.'

'Aren't you going to clear up?'

'No.'

I said no, and I meant it. When the slovenly 'clear up,' the only effect it can possibly have is to accentuate — to put a French polish on — their slovenliness. Plus, the last time I kow-towed to the conventional, the inquisitive and malevolent eyes of Yevgeny saw all. He must have one of those memories that files away each detail until it can be used as malicious entertainment. He probably has one of those memory theatres beloved of the Renaissance magi, Lull and Bruno and Fludd, and placed the inventory of Vanikin's dark solitude in the unshuttered window of some house or pavilion of his mental acquaintance. Part of my sister's reason for this regal attention is to remind herself of her success, carrying the family torch, whatever good she thinks that is going to do her. Arachnadia. The web trembles.

The boy says I have an hour or so before my sister arrives to chill the soul of Europa House, and I spend it musing, remembering, pondering, letting the roll of memory unfurl like a vast carpet let loose at the top of a flight of stairs, unspooling, bumping, and bouncing down to the basement of the past. I sit in my chair and look at what remains of the wallpaper, dreadful Georgian arabesques faded and picked at by whoever had the cell before my expulsion brought me here. I go where my mind takes me, led by the nose through a rusted and clanking penny arcade of time. Back to school.

I attended a grammar school in a Home Counties market town — boys only, school uniforms, satchels, Latin, the type of establishment looked upon by today's educational martinets as some sort of bastion of oppression, like a slave-galley on the rolling seas of the Middle Passage or a Burmese sweat-shop filled with children sewing dreadful items of rapper-endorsed clothing for a few cents and a place to sleep where they wouldn't actually die.

I was a reasonably successful student without ever being liked by the teachers, a joiner-in of schoolboy intrigues without really making any friends, and a competent figure on the sports field without really enjoying myself. I seemed an adult in a child's body, unaware of the licence of youth, waiting only for the time when I could be alone with my one treasure trove, my Elysian field, my constant and unswerving companion. Books.

My, how Vanikin read. Hunched over a Walter Scott novel on the bus, feeling my way through Tennyson in the bath while the water went tepid and my body wrinkled and puffed, probing the ideas of T. H. Huxley while everyone else was at the funfair, I read not like an eager boy but like a Victorian notary, eschewing the fireworks of the standard rite-of-passage novels for the drab and the dour. No *Catcher in the Rye* for Harry — none of that cerebral chewing-gum. I was more likely to be found frowning over Galsworthy or Richardson. It was as though someone from the future — my future — had popped back to inform me that that future was going to be a serious, unfrivolous affair, and I was assembling my mental library accordingly. The world was like a film I had wandered into halfway through and realised not only had I seen it before but it was dull and boring the first time around, and reading was the only escape route. A bookless world, for Vanikin, was as a rungless ladder to the window-cleaner, a bristle-free brush to the painter, a cottonless needle to the seamstress.

I never got into trouble at school, in the local park, at parties. I didn't go to the local park, for a start, which was all dog-shit and lumpen morons kicking footballs at jumpers, or between them, or whatever it is you do. And I certainly didn't go to parties, even if anyone had been socially dysfunctional enough to invite me to one. My parents despaired. They would have cheered a school detention, applauded a black eye, had a memorial plaque made at a bench on which I had vomited a stew of cider and chips. But Vanikin had one eye on the future, which was where he was planning his campaign of mischief and disgrace...

University was simply more of the same. One would think the bookish young adult would be welcomed to the groves of academe as a homecoming princeling, but my encyclopaedic knowledge of Shakespeare, or Locke, or Hardy, or whatever the set seminar text was seemed both to rile my tutors and alienate my fellow students. While other undergraduates stormed the cut-price campus bars after lectures, I went back to the library. I fell asleep there once in a corner, and no one noticed. They closed the library and locked me in. I bedded down between the rows of gorgeous volumes, and when I awoke the next morning ran my fingers over the nearest book's spine as though it were a lover's warm flank.

Master's degree succeeded Bachelor's, and a PhD was a formality. By now, I had relegated literature to the status of a secret love from whom I stole kisses at opportune moments, but I had by then met and married the love of my life: philosophy. She had appeared to me long before my doctorate, like a genii, like the Lady Philosophy manifesting herself in the jail cell of Boethius. I would never be unfaithful; I would never even look at another woman.

I know what you're thinking. Oh, dearie, dearie me. Look at all the *imagery*. Women everywhere in Vanikin's head but never in his bed. Not so. I had my rolls in the hay. Complimented on one occasion on my longevity during the carnal act, I chose not to mention that my stamina was due to the fact that, instead of paying attention to my paramour, I was considering the ways in which Kafka's career as a patent clerk, and the language such a formal and ordered job required, affected his prose style. Despite these occasional coital interruptions, the only covers Vanikin wished to be between had ISBN numbers printed on them. There was, of course, Clara, whom I went so far as to marry. But to quote the poet Shelley, that is a tale for the long winter nights.

My reveries are broken by the boy's warning paradiddle on the door. I know what this means, and I feel naked, mentally unprepared. Quite appropriate, I feel, to have quoted from Percy Bysshe's long poem *The Witch of Atlas*.

My sister is here.

CHAPTER SEVEN

Queen and Consort

My sister's marriage was, as with all the major events of her life, a carefully controlled psychological experiment, her husband being the Estonian ambassador to Paraguay and the only child of a world-renowned pastry chef who had once worked for Kruschev, and a professional tightrope-walker.

Think of how many ambassadors there must be. How many countries are there? Say, two hundred, even including the ones that are barely more than an unweeded backyard full of pig muck. Each has an ambassador to each, no? I know there are zanies like North Korea and Cuba, but still. The best part of forty thousand ambassadors. Do they all hide in their hearts different secrets or the same one? Nadia went to Paraguay with her new husband shortly after their marriage, but she hated the humidity. I'm surprised she didn't just raise a rune-carved staff like Prospero and put an end to it.

Well, she will be here any moment and, if we are going to compare her to the magus of *The Tempest*, then we must extend the metaphor and call her son Yevgeny a dreadful hybrid of both Caliban and Ariel. *Unnatural as thou art...*

I feel like Camus' poor old stranger, waiting for the steps outside his prison cell. Soon enough, even time will not save us now — did time ever save anything save itself? The boy drums the door, and I open it. The raid has begun. The boy is the herald.

'Hello, Mr. Vanikin. Your sister is here to see you.'

Is it me, or is the boy starting to talk to me as though I were back in the TV room? 'Now, Harry. Your *dinner* is here. Yes. Put the remote down, Harry. It's time for your *dinner*.' I am summoned rudely back to the present and its trials.

And there she is, with the fruit of her loins in attendance. She looks like an ambassador herself (ambassadress?) but one to Narnia or Mars or wherever. He is wearing a black suit and white shirt buttoned up to the neck but with no tie. I have never liked this, it is a fashion statement I don't understand, an unreadable semaphore. What's he reading now? Amish literature? A history of Georgian undertaking? The bloody *Torah*? I back off in supplication but remain standing as the pair enter, blood of my blood, flesh of my flesh.

My sister comes in, but I avoid her eyes. I sometimes think I'd be better off looking at Nadia in the reflection of a highly polished shield. I motion her to sit in the guest chair, and she does so, a foreign queen taking the throne of a conquered country, her brother a wretched satrap suppliant under her dominion. Yevgeny, as usual, looks at me and smiles his serial-killer smile. He takes the only other seating available, a rickety dining chair of charity shop provenance. He says,

'And we back away and hide from the light, the beacon to which we ourselves gave fire.'

The little bastard. The *little bastard*. He is quoting from *The Decadent Turn*, quoting from my own damned — oh, so damned — academic *oeuvre*. My sister, sensing this early thrust by her malignant offspring, offers to parry for me.

'Well, Harry. I have your money.'

'Thank you.'

She produces a neat roll of banknotes and passes them to me. Yevgeny smiles, happy to be witness to a transaction which belittles me and establishes his mother's superiority over the situation. Pagan gods alone knew what form this twisted soul's love took, but he loved his mother, like a good boy. Nadia continues.

'I can give you more. You do have money.'

'Why would I want more? I spend the same amount every week.'

'Perhaps you could buy some nice things for this…place.'

Nice things. Fiddlesticks. Lark spit. What nice things? A chaise-longue? An elephant's foot umbrella stand? A lazy fucking Susan for my table, the length of that table's legs equalised against wobbling as they are by a copy of the Everyman edition of Immanuel Kant's *Prolegomena to any Future Metaphysics*? I rejoinder.

'Seneca writes to Lucilius that to make a man rich you must not give him money but lessen his desires.'

'Yes, and it is a good idea, I am sure, to take financial advice from a Roman who has been dead for two thousand years.'

'Not quite.'

'No, not quite. Almost two thousand.'

'I mean he is not quite dead. He lives on in his writing.'

'As I am sure you will in yours.'

'*He's* read it.'

I bucked my silly wrinkled head at Yevgeny like a professional footballer nodding at a crossed ball. The monster speaks.

'Culture cannot be overseen. It is a slave only to itself and has no master.'

I am not to be goaded. Where the hell did he find a copy? A cackling, whooping gang of scarecrow students actually did organise a burning of copies of my book on the university campus. Their dress sense may not have been as creepily elegant as that of the Nazis, but they had read the same playbook. Apparently, they didn't clear up the resultant charred and sopping mess or attend to the scorched grass. The university cleaning team, the Magdas of the ivory towers, had to do that. This is, as is said, where we are now. The young and well-off and shallow of pate have their gurning fun, and the poor clear up after they are done. Nadia exercised once more a diplomacy that she may have learned from her estranged husband. He is back in Estonia, by the way, writing his memoirs and licking his Nadia-inflicted wounds.

'Yevgeny, I think your uncle understands that you have read his book, so we will stop quoting from it now.'

And the monster growls and retreats back into his cave. He sits upright in the chair and gazes straight ahead of him, into what dimension I know not. Yevgeny is not autistic. I doubt that psychology has a name or category for what he is. Perhaps he is the future. Something will evolve from man's present plight — why not him? My sister is trying to reset the situation and introduce order, the type of order she likes.

'How long, Harry, do you intend to stay here?'

'How long have I been here?'

'Seven years and four weeks and three days.'

'I missed my anniversary. I would have baked a cake.'

'You have no oven. You have no shower or bath, either.'

'Do I smell?'

'Only of poverty. And your soul smells.'

Can the soul smell? I recall nothing in Aristotle on the subject, although, of course, we do not have all the Stagirite wrote. There may have been something in the lost work on the olfactory system.

'I don't need those things. I have a room. I have a bed. I have a plate and a bowl and a big spoon and a small spoon and a knife and a fork and a pepper-pot and one of everything except cups, of which I have two. One for me and one for visitors.'

I realise that I am starting to slip into that ticker-tape vocal delivery that had got me into the hospital and fall silent. It's a shame. I have other things, too, but they are all useful, all have a *use*. I don't have a blender or a plasma-screen TV or a computer or a *car* or a phone or a fucking dishwasher. I have what I need, and I need what I have.

'So, still they come.'

'I beg your pardon?'

'Your visitors. Your study group. The poor and dispossessed. They beat a path to the shaman's door still.'

'I talk to people. You will find it is an ordinary human activity. Like shitting and pissing and sleeping.'

'Yes, just like.'

'What good have you done for the community lately, Nadia?'

'Oh, saintliness. Do you absolve them of their sins?'

'No, I listen to them. No one else does.'

'Why don't you charge?'

'You said yourself I have money.'

Nadia winced imperceptibly. I could see that she felt that there had been, if not a palpable hit, at least a graze, a tiny epidermal abrasion.

'I have a room in my house. Come. Live like a normal human being.'

A normal human being. When I last excused myself from the goblin market of the outside world over seven years ago, a normal person was a psychotic, self-obsessed freak dressed in some man-made motley. Vanikin in trainers, perhaps? Vanikin with tattoos and a nose-piercing, sitting in a burger bar with a warped plastic tray of anti-food and a milkshake the colour and consistency of nursery paint?

'This is normal.'

'For some.'

'No. For me.'

'Come out. Don't be afraid of the world. Come and live with us.'

Oooooh, yes. Oh, that would be fine and dandy. Come and live with my sister the archon and her son, who wouldn't have to wait to visit once a month to pick the wings off a fly. I'd rather go back to the hospital and fight with Mr. Pennett about who got more custard on his butterscotch slice.

'I'm not afraid of the world. I seem to remember it is afraid of me.'

'Oh ho! You have a complex! My brother has delusions of grandeur. It takes me right back to the practice, to all those men sitting crunched up in the chair thinking they made any effect on the world when they barely even made a dent in the seat cushion. The world is not afraid of you, pinhead. They pushed you, and you didn't push back, so they kept pushing.'

This is true. True now, true then. The university wouldn't have cared less about my book until the review in one of the Sunday newspapers. The reviewer was a blowsy bitch who wheeled out all the big guns: Colonialism, sexism, unconscious bias, racism, white supremacy, the far-Right. If Enoch Powell had translated *Mein Kampf* into Old Norse, he would have got a milder write-up. This was in the early days of the witch-hunts. I was one of the first dominoes to tumble. Vanikin jeered off campus. Excrement on my study door. Hung in effigy. How do you push back when there is no still surface to push at?

'Someone didn't like me, Nadia.'

'So, you hide. You hide like a child who has been scolded. Are you going to make a comeback, are you plotting your revenge like a comic-book super-villain? Vanikin Man will have his revenge! When you can't control your bladder and your hips crumble, will you stay here? Or will the same nurses take you out who brought you in? You are a patient, Harry. You are an existential cripple. Yevgeny, come.'

She can't be said to walk to the door as she rises regally. She just turns round, really. Kant tells us that space is the condition of the exterior world. Not so much in here. Yevgeny opens his mouth, doubtless to let slip one more barbed excerpt from my work, but Nadia gives him such a withering look I think he may turn to stone and become a permanent fixture, like the animals in the Queen of Narnia's garden. The pair leave wordlessly, Nadia tipping the boy in my sight just to finish the job of establishing the power relations that had set the tone for another pleasant family get-together.

With Nadia, it wasn't a question of watching how she acted and listening to what she said and then trying to tease out an ulterior motive. Ulteriority was her default position. Why would she want to uproot me from *chez* Vanikin? Sisterly love? Please. Some sort of medical experiment? Could I afford a food-taster if I moved in with her? Irrelevant. I had spent seven years and some spare change of days building my castle of ideas here at Europa House, my filigree of words, my interconnections and joined dots and story board of intellectual history, my…sequel?

CHAPTER EIGHT

I am Everywhere Else

The Decadent Turn was accepted for publication and printed by Wilhelmina Books, named for the managing director's mother, who thus became Godmother to both the launch and the torpedoing of my academic publishing career. It was never my intention to set the world on fire, although the student body at my erstwhile university cheerfully extended that metaphor by setting copies of my book on fire, instead.

David Brindell, Wilhelmina's son, organised a launch party and book signing at London's venerable Garrick Club. How times change. Vanikin then, fondling the crystal stem of a wine glass full of an expensive chilled Muscadet while discussing Auguste Comte with a raven-haired female Slavic philosophy student. I felt so saucy that if I had had a moustache, I would almost certainly have twiddled it. And Vanikin now, in the underworld, trying to scrub his tannin-stained and chipped tea-mug, the one with the name and logo of an insurance company on it, the enamel paint worn away in a crescent fitting the slurping mouth of Vanikin. The fall of Mulciber…

The book sold tolerably well, for a first offering from an unknown academic. I was on the radio — the BBC, if you please. Reviews were sound, and my modest offering seemed to contain nothing to displease the gods. *Incipit* Tara Barnes.

Barnes was one of those metropolitan Bacchae who prowl above the city of culture, seeking whom they may devour. Why she was working for one of the most respected Sunday newspapers is beyond my ken. The print press had for years been slowly slipping back into a swamp of irrelevance and insolvency, grasping at root and clump as the sucking ooze gained a purchase on its tired and venerable frame. Their response was to start hiring hacks who had won the meaningless accolade of being 'edgy' in the playrooms of music, fashion, and 'culture' magazines. Requirements for the job were generally a blithe disregard for the finer points of the written word, bad language, and sleeping with one or all of the upper tier of management, either at the newspaper or its parent company or both. And drugs, one imagines, reading their daubs and smears.

A Lovecraftian troll to look at, Barnes was given my book to review despite having no apparent knowledge of philosophy or any discernible academic background. She had written a book of her own, *Bug-Chasing Bitches*, which, I was reliably informed by the people who know about these things, was an account of American prostitutes who deliberately infect themselves with and further incubate the AIDS virus in their pharmaceutically maintained bodies for the benefit of sexual adventurers who actively seek to become infected with that particular disease. What pantheon is this? I was hardly peer-reviewed.

What happened next was very similar to the case of the Danish imams of whom I was informed by Lars, our man in Scandinavia. *Densmarket Magazine* had published cartoons of the Islamic prophet Mohammed — strictly *verboten* under the tenets of that religion — and no one noticed very much. Some time later, two imams in Denmark *did* notice, and something became very rotten in that state very quickly.

Muslims do not stand on ceremony when they feel there is a point of order *vis à vis* their religion to be discussed and brought to the attention of the wider community, and they responded accordingly. Rioting, bloodshed, a full media offensive, attacks on the publisher's premises brought a groveling retraction and yet more self-flagellation from governments across Europe.

The trial of *The Decadent Turn* was even more tenuous. From my intention to present to other scholars a critical examination of academic theory from the Renaissance to the present day, the book was remade as a white supremacist tract, a racist screed, a tool of oppression, and every other label pulled from the semantic box of tricks a certain type of academic has at their disposal.

This ferocious turn of a rabid pack happened to coincide with a new wave of student rebellion. It was Paris '68 and the *soixante-retards* all over again, the Watts riots, Berkeley but against freedom of speech rather than in its defence. *The Decadent Turn* was just the young drummer-boy at the head of the army, mown down by the gunfire that would soon slaughter the troops behind him. None of the book-burners and denouncers had actually *read* the book, but you don't need to do that anymore. The merest hint of a sniff of a suspicion of a rumour, and you are a cross between the Grand Kleagle of the Ku Klux Klan and Sir Oswald Mosley.

I was invited on television to discuss the reaction to the book. Two of the panel immediately refused to share a stage with me, and a third said she would only take part if I was made to stand to one side of the stage and be addressed by the seated inquisitors, a prime-time show trial with after-shave advertisements in between defence and prosecution statements.

And my erstwhile colleagues, each and every one of them, walked away. I would not — I *could* not — apologise for the book, which is what I was asked to do by the university. They wanted me to recant. One of the Student Union gauleiters actually used the word. Recant.

I responded to this sudden earthquake of hatred and death threats and bile and scorching, scourging persecution in the only way I feel an Englishman could decently respond; I went mad.

The day started ordinarily enough. I had a meeting with an inspector from the London Metropolitan Police who confirmed that, although I would not be facing any hate-crime charges, it might be a good idea if I stayed out of the public eye for a while. Then, I had lunch with my publisher, David, at his apartment in Crouch End. He was nervous and fidgety, as though he were lunching with Osama bin Laden in a cave in the Hindu Kush. From there, I went to the offices of a phone-in radio station, where I was interviewed by an amused young lady who seemed to find the whole episode humdrum and run-of-the-mill. Then, I went home. Then, I went mad.

I lived in a pleasant block of flats whose caretaker, the polar opposite of Craig, was busy sweeping up in the yard when I approached him and asked if he could call an ambulance. I was carrying a copy of Diogenes Laertius' *Lives of the Philosophers* and a French baguette, and I was wearing a Venetian masquerade mask which was a souvenir of a party many years previously, its long, red, hooked nose and sculpted eyebrows making me look like a terrible bird. Other than that, I was entirely naked.

Madness is both under- and over-rated. From the moment I was bundled into the ambulance — robed in a too-small gown — and driven to a hospital, I was as happy as a lamb. Once my sister and, of course, the kobold Yevgeny had arrived — why did she let him come? — and confirmed that I was who I said I was — although, as we shall see, that was a moot point at the time and definitely up for grabs — I was strapped to a bed and given some extraordinarily wonderful drugs. Unknown to me, I was then moved to another hospital, now a prisoner of 1983's

Mental Health Act, making me, I suppose, a type of kin of Estrella's. I had, to use Craig McCerrow's phrase, been 'nutted off.'

I had my own little room. As mentioned in a previous episode, Nadia saw to everything. Of course, this was perfect for her, but she didn't let the unscheduled — was it? — arrival of this new game stop her from taking care of me. Some people are excited by the distress of others. Nadia wasn't excited; I have never in my life seen her excited. She just had a new game. *Off* came the shiny paper, *off* came the crêpe paper, open the box, it's perfect and new, no batteries required.

We have seen the television room, and we have met Alex, but the hospital was alive in other ways. I did a lot of thinking. No. Thinking did a lot of me. Philosophy. Philosophy peeled back like a face under autopsy, the sinew and gristle slippy and lickable, underneath another face and beneath another. My sister kept the masquerade mask. A dog ate the bread. I still have the copy of Diogenes Laertius, but I have never dared open it since because I dreamt the words had changed their order.

The dreams began to come when the medication changed. The dreams would not remain in the night. They came with me. Into the day.

Time was everywhere. Space repeated itself and had a slowness that space would have if space were time if three were six were nine. I was in the hospital for a little less than a year. My sister saw to everything. I saw everything.

After a while, everything is medication. Everything has side-effects. Or, rather, everything has effects. One of them is the one you want. Or don't want. The hospital, unknown to everyone inside it, was alive. *I* knew, but, then, there wasn't much I didn't know. I saw it all. You would be amazed how limited the eyes are ordinarily.

When I was released, it was not because of what I told them in the release interview but because of what I didn't tell them. I didn't tell them about the coding, I didn't tell them about the numbering systems, I didn't tell them about the rituals, and I certainly didn't tell them about the dream of the building. Inside the building was where I needed to be, and so, I had to pretend to come up with words I knew would get me out. But they weren't my words; they were lent to me from a long time ago, aeons ago. We do not own words; they own us — or, at least they watch over us. They are guardians, and they announce what is and is not.

I knew where the building was, and I knew how to get there. To move there wouldn't be easy because my sister would want me to live with her, but once I was out, I knew how to persuade her, knew the numbers and the rituals.

They wouldn't give me anything to write with. I understood. The Big Dutchman — that was his only name — stabbed Mr. Pennett with a biro he stole from little Katrina the nurse — as opposed to big Katrina — and so, you could see that the pen was mightier than the sword, at least in a place where there were no swords. I had to wait a long time, watching, hoping for an unguarded moment or move.

Finally, in the night, I knew the words. I wasn't dreaming. I was awake and already inside the house. That day, I had pretended to be asleep in the television room, and Claude had dropped a crayon, and I made it roll, roll, and scuttle under the TV cupboard, that being the cupboard — more of a chest of drawers — that the TV was on. But I got the crayon.

I worked all night, following the segment of moonlight around the walls in accordance both with the numbering system and the ritual of the house and its innards. I chipped down the crayon with my teeth, looking like a hooker besmirched by an evening's frenetic oral sex. I knew that it would take more words, but I had the key, and I made the letters as straight as I could. I didn't know the colour of the crayon, but it knew me because of what I wrote, which would go on to affect many, many people. In the morning, they found me, and I looked up and smiled. My work was done. It said many, many, many times:

I am everywhere else.

CHAPTER NINE

Breakfast of Champions

The passage from the world of sleep and dreams to the tattered tenement of the waking world is, for poor Vanikin, like the transition for the seal emerging from the ocean: graceful, streamlined, and swift while arcing through the water, yet suddenly transformed into a flopping monster making its erratic way up the clinging sand. I usually come round like a coma victim, mind and body engaging slowly and reluctantly, all rusted cogs and off-centre flywheels.

This morning, however, has a bright, almost summery feel to it as I realise, firstly, that I have not been imprisoned in a gulag somewhere and that the monthly symposium with my sister and the creature from the black library is over for another four weeks and a bit. I feel like a racehorse that has got over Beecher's Brook alive and doesn't have to face it again for another full circuit of Aintree racecourse.

It feels early in the day. I grope beneath the bed for my torch, a child's toy in the shape of a dolphin the boy gave me when my last torch succumbed to its Chinese genes. I had asked the boy if he could take it somewhere to be repaired, and he gave me that look, the look the first Dutch settlers at the Cape of Good Hope must have given the indigenous people when they had finished leaping about and genuflecting. Things are not repaired anymore; they are replaced. It is one of the many, many features of the modern world that vex Estrella, who views the world as would a nun view a fly-covered, pot-bellied sub-Saharan infant.

These are the times that try to try men's souls, but cannot, largely due to the comfort blanket of routine. My Flipper torch and I negotiate the short distance to the light switch, and the day is up-and-running, torpedo in the water. Firstly, I perch myself primly on the toilet bowl. I will spare the details, but there is a satisfactory series of small plopping sounds, like fat raindrops in a boathouse, and all is well, my faecal output being traditionally drier than an ecclesiast's sense of humour.

I wash face and hands. I will perform full ablutions later, allowing my body time to regain its composure after another night in the twisted man-made sheets that also serve, and address the kitchen.

The kettle is plopped onto the gas ring, after I have sniffed thoroughly to ensure the gas is inside the canister where it is intended to be. Craig, I am cheerfully informed by Mrs. Podolski, buys these canisters at a cut price, although still charges us at the full rate, and every now and again, one suffers a faulty valve, as law student Mr. Mkambe G'Pono discovered one morning when, on lighting his cooker, he was blown backwards through the Gyproc partition and onto the bed of his neighbour, the octogenarian Mrs. Philps, who may have believed her randy old prayers to have been answered. The two are actually firm friends now, and I suppose that, as a gesture of introduction, appearing in a sheet of flame through someone's wall has something to be said in its favour.

And now — this is Vanikin as tour guide, TV presenter of some palaeolithic settlement or burial mound — we move on to the porridge stage of the morning. Firstly, the saucepan, which has no handle and should be grasped with the Care Bear oven glove, must be placed centrally on the Formica work surface. Formica. Who came up with that design classic? And why bother to *decorate* it, for Christ's sake? Formica always has a stupid little design all over it, like tiny crazy-paving. What's the point? To brighten up the place? That's like wallpapering a condemned cell. And why is it called Formica? Was that its inventor's name, like Hoover or Biro? The Hungarian, Laslo Biro. Tired of quill, chalk, charcoal, even the fountain-pen, deciding the world's scribes needed bringing into the twentieth century, when mankind — although it didn't realise it at the time — was so much happier in the nineteenth. Quite clever, though, the sliver of plastic tubing filled with its staining goo. A sudden flash of little boys at school placing the biros of their enemies on a radiator in winter, the result, mess and uncleanable horror. Little boys. A Waffen SS in miniature.

The saucepan strategically placed, the porridge now makes its entrance on the bright day. The box it comes in has a picture of a man, presumably of the Caledonian persuasion, smiling happily as he prepares to propel a huge sphere to destinations unknown and out of shot. He is wearing a kilt. Do people actually wear kilts? I mean, apart from to weddings when they discover that one of their great-great uncles was vaguely Scottish, and they feel the need to rekindle the spirit of the fighting man. The kilted Vanikin, striding with a broadsword across the heather, a lassie and a suckling bairn to defend from the sassenach. Hoots. Did any Scot, ever, say hoots? You see, now, why I chose philosophy. The world generates questions, endless questions.

Half a cup of porridge is the recommended amount. This is leavened with salt, less than a quarter of a teaspoon, more than an eighth, always the same to the practised and expert Vanikin eye. Next, a cup and a half of water, a quick stir with the spatula — another strange word; did someone invent it? Count Spatula? — and the whole to be left for five minutes — for which I have an ancient egg-timer — stirring occasionally to ensure a smooth consistency.

Routine, the quotidian march of the bachelor's day, very much meets with my approval. I missed it in the hospital. That's one thing about being mad. People do all the little things for you. It's the big problems they can't help you with. *I am everywhere else…*

While I am waiting for the porridge to marinade, I consider my working program for the day. I usually pluck a magazine at random from the bath to get the juices roiling. Mrs. Philps was having a clearout — some time before, she had to deal with incoming in the shape of a flying and singed M'kambe — and had the boy drop the magazines off with me, as she thought I would 'like a nice read.' You may think a once-tenured professor of the discipline which was once theology's handmaiden would sneer at this offer and reject the tawdry collection, but you would be wrong. These women's magazines, gardener's almanacs, and dress-making catalogues from the 1960s onwards are treasure trove to the genuine seeker after knowledge. I would take a *Reader's Digest* account of a visit to a Neolithic flint museum in Wiltshire over Hobbes' fucking *Leviathan* any time of day or night.

The porridge is now ready for the heating process, the laboratory of Vanikarius the Renaissance alchemist is bubbling away nicely. I use the wooden spoon, scarred with small blackened pock-marks like a Bantu initiate, and stir regularly. When this nutritious and toothsome broth is ready, and the Care Bear oven glove in place, it is poured into the bowl, which also serves as a soup bowl and a dessert bowl, before having a heaped spoon of Demerara sugar plopped in and stirred. A dash of cold milk, and the whole now resembles the sort of industrial-strength epoxy I once saw my father slathering onto a wall preparatory to hanging wallpaper. I eat a bowl of porridge every day, with scant heed to the turning seasons, and to it, I attribute my longevity thus far.

This kingly repast dispatched, and feeling inclined as a result neither to don a kilt nor hurl a huge iron globe out of the window, I settle into a magazine article, which concerns the cross-breeding of the terrier dog. I have little experience of the domesticated dog — or, for that matter, the cat. Of the two, and were I forced to play host to one or the other, I believe I would plump for the feline. Dogs seem to view every event as if it were, by far and away, either the best thing that has ever happened to them or to any other dog in history, or the worst. Cats, on the other hand, exhibit an agreeable Stoicism, exuding a clear sense that they have many better things to do than keep the company of humans, but none of those options press with any urgency.

Well, my *pourparlers* over within the realm of the literary, I deem a cup of tea essential. I place the kettle on its infernal ring and insert a tea-bag into the insurance mug noted in a previous episode. I once tried one of Estrella's 'herbal' teas. These things are more expensive than the rustic English tea I usually consume, and are exemplary of the stupidity of a generation of people who believe that the promotion of individual health involves expenditure, and the more the better. I will not describe the taste as there was none to describe, the tea-bag having imparted at most a light urinary colour to the water and presumably having an effect taking place within the remit of the homeopathic.

Under no circumstances are you to stroll off down your personal boulevard with the impression that I am shirking my duties to the muse, the Lady Philosophia. I'll none o' that. Sorry, that's the porridge talking. Much like my choice of magazine led me this merry morn to the world of terrier breeding, so, too, will I choose at random from my extensive bathroom library. At present, I am rudderless, a man without a plan, an anti-systematiser. Never trust systems. Descartes with his rebuilding of experience from the crazy-house of universal doubt, Spinoza with his ethical dominoes, Hegel with his sodding spirals of history. No system for Vanikin, he is a curse on and a snook cocked at systems. Systems are what got me here in the first place, not that I plaint. Systems got me here in two senses, actually, and don't think I haven't spotted your raised eyebrows and sucked-in cheeks of disbelief. You should see yourselves in the mirror. Not only did my attempt to join historical dots lead to me being the Savonarola of the twenty-first century, burnt at the stake of political correctness, it was also a system — a sort of sequel to my full bout of madness, a keepsake from the hospital — that led me here to Europa House.

Because that's what you want to ask, isn't it? Be honest, it's still possible. If, as my sister has correctly pointed out on many occasions, I am not short of a bob or two, why am I not living in comparative ease and even luxury? Why not some rooftop pad, floor-to-ceiling windows which darken their tint in the summer, dove-tailed wooden flooring made from blonde Scandinavian ash, vast pot-plants with leaves as big as the welcoming arms of a woman? Vanikin padding around in linen and expensive socks, a silk robe, and an expensive scotch in hand?

Because I was meant to be here. The first time I saw it — apart from in the dream — I was walking abroad to escape the microscope slide of my sister's flat, my first stop after the hospital, and took a turn unknown to me. And there it was. Europa House seemed like something from my future, a protruding angle from the fourth dimension jutting into our own paltry three, a destiny in brutalist battleship grey. I knew I had to live there.

I wandered in and was soon accosted by Craig, whose

instinct for the unwanted individual honed over two decades as a doorman did not desert him. He seemed to say,

'Fiyuwa?'

This was, in a sort of demotic, *ad hoc*, Anglo-Saxon, pig-English, if you will, an enquiry as to my reasons for having paid Europa House this peremptory visit.

'Well,' I said. 'I'd like to live here.'

CHAPTER TEN

Time and the Maiden

Curious that the great insights can come to a thinker while he is performing the most mundane of tasks. Nietzsche tells us, through his comedy moustache as well as through the misty bead curtain of time, that his best ideas were 'won by walking.' Easy to say when you go for your morning stroll in the Upper Engadine. I doubt that *Thus Spake Zarathustra* would have been much of a read if Fred had had to stroll down to Ahmed's 7/11 each morning for fags and tinned ravioli, avoiding dog-shit and nutters en route.

In my case, the realisation that I might be foolishly toying with a sequel to *The Decadent Turn*, entitled — as I am sure you have guessed — *I am Everywhere Else*, was taking me away from my real philosophical purpose came while I was trying to mend the tin-opener. These devices used to be straightforward, looking like great metal insects momentarily resting on some trembling leaf, but now they have added extra plastic covers and baffling hidden mechanisms. Why does the world change and allow itself to be changed when it worked perfectly well to begin with? Who are the confounders, the obstructors of what could be a simple life? But I digress, trigress, multigress. What, O Vanikin (I hear you implore), is your purpose, of which you have been so wilfully neglectful?

Why, my people.

My children?

An interesting theory, but not, I think, one that translates into practice. I never had children for two main reasons. One, I would have made a lousy father, what with my insular life choices and — as it transpired — general mental instability. Two, I never needed them. Some people require children to satiate an atavistic need, a tugging deep in the mammalian brain and loin. Not Vanikin. He has the ghosts and sprites of his mind, what poor old rat-faced Kafka called 'the incredible world I hold inside my head,' to fill a strange and over-subscribed nursery.

No, they are my people. Europa House is my calling. And, do you know? I believe the first of the day is here. It is, as it almost always is, Estrella, Our Lady of the Cardigans.

I let her in, and she slips between the door and the 'wall' like the ghost of a ghost, a spectre's residue. She sits in the guest chair, her knees primly together, like her hands. I offer 'tea.' Sorry, but today, when things in the objective real world fail to come up to the promise and premise of the word that signifies them, I will use inverted commas. I suppose I could go full Heidegger and write ~~tea~~ or ~~wall~~. Estrella agrees to this social transaction, and I reheat the trusty kettle. She is, as always, perturbed. Perturbation is her natural habitat, her default position, the quo of her status. She speaks in a doomed sigh.

'They're dealing drugs again, Harry.'

As breaking news goes concerning the colourful world of narcotics and its attendant economy, Estrella is more or less sitting in the newsroom with the anchor. The regular presence of Marek, Declan, Marvin M., and Bertie Spedding in my humble abode speaks irresistibly of the presence of a drug empire at Europa House, and quite possibly makes me an accessory after the fact. I say,

'Who is?'

'Oh, you know. The boys upstairs. And RoMarlon. And I

know what you're thinking. It's not because he's a person of colour.'

A few points here. Firstly, Estrella's claim to 'know what I am thinking' is not only absurd in the obvious sense, but fanciful even as conjecture. Even *I* don't know what I'm thinking most of the time, and I'm the one thinking it, standard Husserlian criticisms of the Cartesian *cogito* notwithstanding. Secondly, drug-dealing is to Europa House what herring-fishing is to Lars' native Denmark and the production of the Arabica coffee bean to various Latin American countries, an irreplaceable and undeniable economic fact. Thirdly, what is it with this 'person of colour' business? Is there a person *not* of colour? How do we register their existence, equipped as we are with the standard organs of vision? RoMarlon is, as his name might conjure and as my sister might say, as black as your hat. He rejoices under the familiar name of 'Skunk Daddy.' I say,

'Well, Estrella, you could always go to the police.'

This is very naughty of me, I know. Even the British police would find RoMarlon a person of interest in terms of the sheer quantity of drugs he has at his disposal. Declan, who has been inside this cannabis sultan's inner sanctum, declared it a 'weed warehouse.' If Estrella were to lead the forces of law and order — wait, ~~law~~ and ~~order~~ — to RoMarlon's retail outlet, even they would be pressed to find a reason not to arrest him.

But, for Estrella, RoMarlon is not a black drug dealer. He is an oppressed person of colour whose ancestors sang moving spirituals as they filled hempen bags with raw cotton, always under the watchful eye and stinging whip of the white master. Estrella's generation has played an extraordinary trick with the idea of attributes, eschewing obvious reality in favour of a deep and sacrosanct myth. It is almost Homeric. She herself cannot see that the problem of which she complains is also a network of problems she herself defends. She says,

'It's not just him. Boys come in off the street.'

Well, my poor silly little sweetpea, of course, they do. You were too busy imbibing cultural Marxism at the local sausage-factory they have mis-named a 'university' to know anything of the simple principles of economics, which begins with the happy marriage of supply and demand, followed by supplementary supply chains. That is, lads queue to purchase RoMarlon's apparently premium product, and what they don't smoke themselves they sell to other drug users at a mark-up or 'surplus value,' to use the Marxist term. I say,

'Well, as long as you keep away from them, and keep away from drugs, you will be fine.'

Hardly Confucian, I grant you, but Estrella seems to find some solace therein. I make her fractionally chemically altered hot water, noting its provenance in woodland and field cheerily. I want to ask her if she has ever had a real cup of tea, ever eaten proper food instead of the vegan slop she eats and which contributes to her obvious malnutrition, ever gone out drunk and had a proper fuck in the woods. But I could never do that to Estrella. She is too fragile. Even the harsh angles of the world I have seen are not to be introduced to her delicate worldview. She says,

'How was your sister?'

I think, silently: Superior. Aloof. Cold. Patronising. Distant. Empty. Callous. Charmless.

'Fine.'

'Does she still want you to move back in with her?'

'She does, actually.'

And then, the world took me by surprise, tripped me from behind, bopped me on the base of the skull with a rubber black-jack. Estrella looks at me with something in her eyes, and says,

'Don't go. Don't move in with her. We all want you to stay. We need you.'

I turn my face quickly to one side, like someone on the receiving end of a powerful slap which, I suppose, is exactly what I am. Estrella can see. In that wrenched and wretched second, she can see the link, the dreadful glue that binds us in our despair, the tears that irrigate the world of the lonely. These are our chains, this our poor island cell. Estrella gets up quickly, embarrassed and upsetting her ~~tea~~, which, it occurs to me, might actually help clean the carpet, thereby pleasing Magda and keeping the universal equilibrium equilibriate. Estrella tosses out a couple of strangled phonemes for my consideration and exits stage left. I throw myself on the battered bed, cry for twenty minutes, and collapse into sleep.

When I wake, it is quiet. I can just make out the humming of the great beast of Europa House, the pipes and the wires and the boilers and the settlements and movements of old architecture. I get up and make tea and sit and think about the human condition.

What brought us to this pass? Yes, the history of *homo sapiens* is Graeco-Roman culture and the Renaissance and the Enlightenment and the printing-press and the Industrial Revolution and Dante and Shakespeare and Beethoven. But it is also tired old men weeping on failing cheap furniture in rabbit-hutches off the ring-road. Move from spade to shovel, the pit is dug. It's time to load on the earth, rattling the coffin lid and ready for the rain which always will fall.

Estrella shouldn't be leading this life, shouldn't be here among the misfits and human oddities. She should be out having fun, meeting men, drinking fruity cocktails and dancing. What is she, twenty-five? And already old. Me, I was old before I could walk, I was born old. Vanikin is transmigration gone awry. But she doesn't deserve her time to be served out of joint. Oh, sweet Jesus, don't tell me I am getting a muse, Raskolnikov's Sonya in a fake pearl-button cardi.

I pick up a book and leaf through it, and after two or three minutes, I realise it is upside-down. Appropriate. Topsy-turvy, arse about face, widdershins and *contra mundum*, like Vanikin. That's why I'm down here and not up there. Vanikin in the underworld. And Eurydice? I can't think these thoughts. I cut a slice of Swiss roll to have with my tea. What time is it? This is ridiculous. I can't rule time but refuse to have a clock. I must have a clock. An idea forms so wholly, and so immediately, it is like being mugged by a Jack-in-the-box.

I will ask Estrella to get me a clock. She loves charity shops and dresses exclusively from their off-the-rail oddities and kooky couture. Charity shops have clocks, old clocks, carriage-clocks, plastic 1950s jobs with skinny Roman numerals and a long, gliding second hand, analogue railway clocks whose second-hands click and clunk, making space out of time. 'Time,' says Kant, 'is the necessary form of our internal intuitions,' the condition of all experience in cahoots with its sibling, space. This is why Vanikin suffers and floats and spins in the ether, in free-fall, a free-for-all, because he has rejected time and must bring it back into the fold.

I will ask Estrella to buy me a charity-shop clock, one with a second-hand second-hand. The Americans call charity shops 'thrift stores.' Thrifty Vanikin. What would be the budget? Ten pounds? A hundred? What price time? I will ask Estrella what she thinks. Already, I feel a sea-change, a shifting of the tectonic plates of routine. This is what I need, something new and different; Vanikin gets a re-think, change and change again, new balls please.

I eat the last little strip of Swiss roll — I always unwind a Swiss roll and lay it across the oblong plate, which is, in reality, the base of a butter dish whose lid I broke long ago — and finish my tea, washing up immediately. I never allow even one item of washing-up to collect. For the bachelor, setting his tilt at the world alone, a pile of washing-up is the final and authentic emblem of defeat.

My world was about to change, and the alterations would be of my making and design. Not only will I not go gently into that good night, I don't even know if it is night, and that is because I have no clock, and that is why I am going to charge Estrella with a quest. Go out and make your circle in the world, O Estrella, and return not until ye have found time.

CHAPTER ELEVEN

The Wonders of the Invisible World

See Vanikin, see his new sense of purpose, a shiny *telos* straight from the factory, changing the tack of his life one nautical degree at a time. With a clock, I will rejoin humanity, *humanitas*, partake in the *sensus communis*, share in the fate and world of others. *You must learn to share, Harry…*

I'm not fudging the issue. I'm not avoiding it, either. Estrella took me by surprise; I cannot tell a lie. Well, I can, and do and have and will, but not on this occasion. That little lachrymal excursion came out of the blue, like sickness or madness. Was I wanted? Did Europa House sing of the hidden king in its songs and odes, its oral tradition? Or was the poor girl just being fanciful? Pah! There are clocks to be bought. Time. There is a rap on the door. Pock. Pock. Pock. Evenly spaced, not one of my regulars. I call softly, and, in supplication that I am not addressing the dreadful and talented mimic Adam, receive a strident and well-known reply. It is Mrs. Pallis. It really is. I don't believe even Adam could replicate the *basso profundo* voice. I open the door.

Mrs. Pallis is a large black lady, always dressed as though she is just going to or coming from church, which is, in fact, often the case. If the Lord moves in mysterious ways his wonders to perform, Mrs. Pallis will be the first to know. To call her devoutly religious would be like calling Ignatius Loyola a bit strict or Caligula a wee bit over the top. We complete our mutual greetings, and Mrs. Pallis turns sideways in a practiced move in order to gain ingress to my dwelling, she being that confusing mixture of huge and yet not grossly, uncontrollably fat. Once inside, and both wary of past organisational and structural false moves and errors, Mrs. Pallis sits her bulk on my sofa, while I take the guest chair which, were it animated, as in a Disney cartoon, would have breathed a sigh of relief. I say,

'Would you like a cup of tea, Mrs. Pallis?'

'You are a darlin', Mr. Vanikin, but noooo, thank you!'

At this point, I will dispense with the exclamation mark at the end of Mrs. Pallis' sentences. Just assume there is one unless notified otherwise. I sit and look expectantly, waiting for Mrs. Pallis' petition, as I sense this is not a social call. This is not to say that Mrs. Pallis does not make social calls. She very much does. When Mrs. Pallis does anything, she does it very much, but she represents a sadly neglected strand of Christianity, the loose and pulled stitch that leads to that elusive milk that is of human kindness.

'Tis about Jimmy-Shawn I have come.'

Much, I would wager, has been said on the subject of Jimmy-Shawn, Mrs. Pallis' errant grandson, by shattered teacher and neurotic parole officer, enervated police constable and disbelieving juvenile magistrate. Jimmy-Shawn is a force of nature. In Ancient Greece, he would have been some sort of Homeric agent of chaos and mischief.

'Is he in trouble again, Mrs. Pallis?'

'Not dis time. Me want to keep him OUT of trouble.'

Capital letters are the only way to express the way that the occasional word leaps from Mrs. Pallis' control like an unfed mastiff at a riot. She continued.

'Im need a job.'

Oh, lord, no. Does she think I can employ Jimmy-Shawn? Vanikin the pit-boss, the *komptroller*, giving employment to a demonic apprentice. Or perhaps she saw me as a sort of academically inclined Fagin, with my little crew of pick-pockets and cut-purses. Ah. No. There is more.

'Im need a seee veee.'

'Ah. I *see*.'

Yes, I did see. Producing a *curriculum vitae* for Jimmy Shawn would require imaginative skill in the art of the hoax on a par with *The Protocols of the Elders of Zion*.

'Is it possible, Mr. Vanikin? Can you 'elp me 'elp 'im?'

Vanikin, I think, you cannot turn one down. If you do, you turn them all down.

'When can he come and see me, Mrs. Pallis?'

Her face, it has to be said, is not merely lit up, it was the physiognomic equivalent of an airstrike on a Vietnamese jungle. She said, seemingly close to tears,

'You are a saint, Mr. Vanikin.'

Perhaps I am. After all, I am getting delusions of grandeur like menopausal beldames get hot flushes, why not go the full nine yards and throw in beatitude, as well? Saint Vanikin of Gyproc, my bones mouldering in Rome's Basilica. Mrs. Pallis finalises details.

'I bring 'im tomorrow at 2:00 p.m. Oh. Oh. God BLESS you.'

Mrs. Pallis negotiates my door in reverse, literally, going out backwards like the successful supplicant I suppose she was and beaming like a sparkling clean dinner plate. I sit back in my old chair and sip at my cold tea. Jimmy Shawn. I was going to earn my canonisation. Oh, balls. I forgot to ask Mrs. Pallis to see if she could send Estrella along. No more prevaricating, Vanikin! Prevanikating. I want my clock, and I want it done. If t'were done when t'were done, t'were best t'were done sharpish.

Never mind. All good clocks to he who waits.

Something is afoot. Am I dying? I'm acting like one of those batteries that, just before they fade away forever, have one last hurrah, a final fling before the rubbish bin. It feels as though something is forming in what Marcus Aurelius — kind, thoughtful old Marcus, with his bitch of a wife — called 'the great web of the universe.' Well, I suppose it was. My immediate future, I would do well to remember, featured the one-boy civil war that was Jimmy-Shawn Pallis.

Jimmy-Shawn had already served time in a juvenile prison that spat him out again like a bad oyster, having schooled his already impressive criminal skills as these places are wont to do. He and his little 'postcode gang' of barely pubertal desperadoes who, at present, limit their out-of-school activities to minor theft and the trafficking of narcotics that so exercised Estrella — clock! — but would, with a grim inevitability, soon graduate to the upper echelons of street crime and its attendant weaponry. To save Jimmy-Shawn from this would, of course, be a laudable thing to do. But could anyone do it, least of all creaky old hermit Vanikin? We would see tomorrow.

Crime. In my lifetime, it has gone from being the province of criminals of adult age to the profession of children, the older criminal classes having the herd thinned by the twin environmental factors of jail and death. And you had to try relatively hard to get a custodial sentence for street crime, and when you did, it just meant a holiday-camp stay, with lots of TV and more drugs.

But to keep Jimmy-Shawn from what looked like pre-destination? Earn your keep, Vanikin! Many are called, but few are chosen. I had forgotten to ask Mrs. Pallis what the job was that her grandchild was hoping would keep his life and liberty on the rickety rails on which they ran. It was, I surmised sadly, unlikely to offer a pension, company gymnasium and full healthcare. And yet, it was odd how many entirely worthless jobs, jobs that are of no genuine use to anyone save the person carrying them out, did offer these glittering prizes. Ah, me. This is no time to ponder on social justice. May as well guess which type of cream cheese the moon is made of. Cream cheese. Time for dinner.

At one time, my sister wanted me to have a microwave, but Vanikin put down his Amish foot, drew a line in the sand, and said 'thus far and no further!'. Microwaves, indeed. I, like the medieval mind, am afeared of the invisible world. Won't have it in the house. *I am the boy who can enjoy invisibility…* Where did that come from, what corner of the cave of memory? Joyce? Yes, *Ulysses.* Joyce, with his NHS specs and his stupid hat. Why couldn't he just write stories about Dublin? Why all the language-mangling? *Finnegan's Wake? Finnegan's Wank.* Anyway, I like a source of heat I can see, out in the open, hands on the car.

So, none of those ready meals in their plastic coffins and gauzy covers for Vanikin. Invisibility is as much of a danger now as it was for Martin Luther, hurling his ink bottle at a devil he couldn't see but knew to be there. Invisible things are sinister, the left-hand path of knowledge. The Kantian noumenon, the Freudian unconscious, the Lockean primary quality, dark matter, Riemannian geometry, Lepton spin. Can't see any of the blighters, but there are people with letters after their name who claim they exist. There's one more. Oh, yes. God. Less said about him the better.

So, then. Half a tin of corned beef, cut into slices not too thick and not too thin, and laid expertly across the plate like a card shark laying down five aces. Next, half a tin of baked beans, which are to the British what rice is to the Chinese, are added. A small tin of string beans take up the corned beef's other flank, the tin drained and the green slivers lying like willow reeds thrown by a reader of the venerable *I Ching*. Finally, mashed potato, conjured from the wallpaper paste in the sachet by the simple addition of water. A dollop of brown sauce completes a colour pallet of which Walter Sickert would have been proud, and a pinch of salt adds seasoning and gives Vanikin the only staff he ever needs, that of life. Dinner is served!

Over dinner, with which I have a glass of the very drinkable tap-water they do here, pre-chilled in the refrigerator, which somehow keeps going despite its age, like a TV gameshow host doing the holiday-camp circuit, I think about my role at Europa House, urban guru, shambling shaman, sink-estate Delphic oracle. In my seven years here, I have advised, sympathized, and psychoanalysed, written letters for the unlettered, signed passport applications for the stateless, and generally been available for the cast here assembled. I have only had two requests to keep items; one denied, one agreed to.

Declan arrived one rainy evening wearing only one training shoe and asked me with some sense of urgency to look after some species of duffel-bag for him. I looked at him with as stern a look as I could muster, which probably made me look like a lollipop-lady with a hidden sorrow, and told him no. It seemed not to affect our relationship, and the next time I saw him, he did not mention the rebuff. That said, Declan's memory is like one of those looped video surveillance tapes that used to be used for store security, wiped and replaced every hour or so. The only time I agreed to keep something in my hutch was when the supplicant was Marvin M.

Marvin M. is the only human here of whom Craig is physically afraid. That is all ye know, and all ye need to know. A black colossus, as wide as he is tall, and always impeccably dressed, Marvin is a drug dealer and a pimp. This is his profession. He probably makes more money than an accountant — indeed, he employs one — and lives at Europa House not for reasons of economy, but for other, rather more mysterious reasons. But that is for another day. He announced himself one day with a sharp rap on my door.

'Mr. Vanikin?'

His voice was smooth and low.

'Could I ask you to look after something for me? Circumstances require me to visit home.'

Home was Jamaica.

'Why, certainly,' I replied to the man-mountain, carrying as he was an immaculate cream-coloured hat-box tied with purple ribbon.

That box sat on my table for five days. It was far too light to contain a human head, and I gained relief from that. By the sixth day, I could no longer restrain myself. I put on a pair of white silk gloves I had inadvertently stolen from the ancient manuscript section of the British Library, carefully undid the bow, and removed the lid to gaze terrified at the contents.

It was a hat.

Chapter Twelve

The Life and Times of Jimmy-Shawn Pallis

Time. Now there's a great leveller. The world is always stamping its little foot and crying out for justice and equality, and it has already been arranged. 'I just don't have time,' we say. Yes, you do, very much so. We all have. We measure time, of course, using space, which is a cosmic category mistake God probably still has his top people working on. Zeno's famous paradox, whereby Achilles' arrow, fired unerringly at its target, never actually strikes that target. Why? Because first it has to travel half the distance between Achilles and that target. But first, it has to travel half *that* distance. But first... 'Time is something I understand perfectly,' writes Saint Augustine, 'until someone asks me to explain it.' You cannot calculate time using space, but we do. Old Kant, with his daily walk so punctual that the good burghers of Königsberg set their clocks by him, comes back to time, time, and time again in *The Critique of Pure Reason*, describing it as a drawn line. Until today, I would have had no clock to set by the old philosopher. Not anymore. I am living in a new time.

I have to confess I didn't believe Estrella was up to the task. She seems to descend into an existential crisis when I ask her which of her nugatory teas she would like while she is on one of her daily visits, so specific instructions and commission of money — I gave her a budget of £20, and two £10 notes *in actualitas* — I had thought might have thrown her into some terrible loop of indecision, like a female Hamlet in a mental Elsinore of her own construction. Faithless Vanikin.

Estrella went on her mission like an eager girl-scout given a detail by Akela. I felt a momentary pang of guilt about sending her out onto the city streets, which felt a little like dispatching Anne Frank to buy me some pork scratchings from a Munich *bierkeller* in 1933, but not half an hour later, she returned not only with the most delightful time-piece, but £8.50 in change to boot. She refused my offer of payment for her trouble, doubtless having been informed by the literature she favours that taking money from a man is tantamount to betraying the sisterhood into the service of a grim-faced and domineering patriarchy. We even set the clock up together, myself setting the metal hands to the correct time and setting it to that shown on Estrella's mystifying mobile telephone.

My temporal knight's lady was not without one of her usual Rolodex of concerns concerning Europa House, however. Estrella had a multitude of worries concerning the place she calls home, as we all do. For her, it is absolutely not a case of 'home, sweet home,' but rather, 'home, source of constant and nagging fears, doubts, concerns, disgust, and disapproval.' Today's plaint is actually one of recent provenance revisited.

'He's still measuring. But guess what?'

'He is using imperial rather than metric?'

She is referring, of course, to the newcomer at this El Dorado, the man who arrived with no belongings save, apparently, a tape measure.

'No. He talked to Craig.'

Well, I thought, I hope he has brought with him either a translator or an anthropological study of primitive tribes, because Craig's speech inflections are taxing to those of us used to standard English usage. I give but one example. When Craig lumps his huge fist on the door and shouts what appears to be 'Waldorf grey towers!', you are, if you are used to these bombastic snippets of information, informed that the water will be going off for eight hours that day. The time of the outage is never, ever specified, nor, as noted in a previous episode, is the time-frame given ever adhered to, and always exceeds that stated. I say flippantly,

'Perhaps they have a mutual interest. Dressage or Balzac or something.'

'Well, Craig is scared of him! He called him 'Sir!''

In much the same way that people have come, in the main, to mistrust the media in terms of its reflection of reality, so, too, Estrella's pronouncements on the affairs of state within Europa House should usually be taken not just *cum grano salis*, but with a whole bushel of the bloody stuff. But this interested me strangely. A human being here — apart from Marvin M., who would not be scared of a horde of Visigoths who had taken a wrong turn at Transylvania — who had managed to place the iron grip of fear on Craig was a force to be reckoned with, and I file this away mentally in the appropriate cranial file, if the head is, indeed, the house of the mind, as seems reasonable to suppose it is, and, besides, there is not time to go into cortical theory here. Time.

I feel its master now. I feel like Dr. Who. Now. The clock must have pride of place *chez* Vanikin. But, where? Most of my books are in the bathroom, but there is a bookshelf in the dining and living area fashioned from an old wooden crate which, its ancient and peeling label informs a waiting world, had once held a consignment of plantain, that Jamaican staple that mimics the banana so authentically that I had once eaten one in error. Books are piled on top, sideways, but it does seem precarious as a perch for my new acquisition, although not, as a concerned Estrella had warned, likely to be dislodged by an earthquake. I informed Estrella that, London being very much neither in California nor Panama, the chance of such an eventuality was remote. As soon as I said it, however, I remembered the way the flimsy superstructure of my cigar-box habitation would shake when either Craig or Marvin M. walked in. Estrella, in a way she knew not, had a point. The floor aside, that had pretty much exhausted the options when it came to horizontal surfaces, discounting the floor, and so, I place it centrally on the table, its fine dark wooden cowl even matching the umber tablecloth. Time. Time!

It is three minutes to two o'clock, and, with a sense of fate reminiscent of Beethoven's 5th, there comes a firm rap on the door. Let lying commence.

It is, pre-punctual, Mrs. Pallis and her grandchild Jimmy-Shawn. I say,

'Ah! Hello! Do come in.'

Mrs. Pallis ushers in Jimmy-Shawn first and then makes her negotiated entrance. Again, naturally now and cogniscent of the structural problems arising from sitting in the guest chair, Mrs. P. takes my throne, while I gesture Jimmy-Shawn into the guest chair, not before his grandmama has sternly prompted him to shake my hand, which he does in a slightly wide-eyed way, and say hello, which he does with remarkably little in the way of standard West Indian verbal pyrotechnics. I am left with the inferior guest's seat. I sit and say,

'Now! How can I help?'

'Well, Jimmy-Shawn. Do you want me to do all de talkin', or will you ask Mr. Vanikin, nicely, what it is you would like his help wid?'

The boy looks at the wall as though there were an apparition there, and says,

'Um, I needs a job, and—'

'NEED!'

This is, of course, Mrs. Pallis. Jimmy-Shawn is going to speak the King's English on her watch; that much is established.

'I *need* a job, and dey want me, my, um, details.'

'I see. A CV.'

Perhaps the boy thinks I am just throwing out random letters of the alphabet, because he looks at me oddly. Mrs. Pallis says,

'Do you know what a seeee-veeee is, Jimmy-Shawn?'

The boy does not.

'Mr. Vanikin,' the lady continues, as though she has just guessed the murderer in a game of Cluedo.

'Well, it stands for something in Latin.'

'LATIN! Oh my!'

This from Mrs. P, sounding like the Church fathers admonishing Erasmus, but actually speaking in tones of reverence, of which she, as a regular church-goer — probably more so than Erasmus — thoroughly approves. And so, we proceed through the afternoon, building a life for young Jimmy-Shawn cut not precisely from whole cloth, but from whatever rags and tattered strips we could find. Interestingly, Mrs. Pallis will not stand for outright fabrication, but embellishment meets with her beaming approval. So, because Jimmy-Shawn had swept the church a couple of times as punishment for social anarchy, we have him as working for that august institution, part-monk, part Knight Templar. An interest in the past exploits of his football team sets him up as something of an amateur historian. His great love of his little sister, Qaneesha, casts him in the role of carer. And that, as Proust noted, is how history gets written.

When we have completed Jimmy-Shawn's testimonial, Mrs. Pallis sends the boy packing back to tend to smiling little

Qaneesha, exhorting him not to let her near any sweet comestibles, but she remains for a *post scriptum*. It is then that she drops the big one.

'Mr. Vanikin,' she begins, moist-eyed, 'many have been called, but few are chosen.'

I have heard the phrase before, of course. The path of saintliness, the taking of orders, he for God, she for God in him, that sort of thing. But setting up Jimmy-Shawn as a latter-day saint on the sole basis of a largely fabricated *resumé*, as our American cousins term a CV, is a bit rich. Mrs. P's sermon, however, is merely in its prefatory stages.

'Mr. Vanikin, I have had cause to see great men doing God's work. Give me the child, and I will give you the man.'

Oh, muffins. She wants to make a Jesuit out of the boy. I couldn't see Jimmy-Shawn, in his shining white laceless trainers, wearing a cassock the colour of my clock's case and illuminating the works of St. Jerome. More, still.

'That little boy is heading down de wrong ROAD! His friends steer him wrong. He walks a path, and at the end of that path, the DEVIL is waiting!'

Actually, I began by being scared that Jimmy-Shawn would steal my clock. Now, I am concerned that his grandmother is going to steal my soul.

'All dese boys need is a firm hand and GUIDANCE! Dey do not see a shepherd because they do not know where to look, Mr. Vanikin. Television. Drugs. Girls who are still girls. Rap music. These are the devil's trinkets. Our work is to keep dem hidden away, but everywhere, they lie for all to see. But the devil is afraid of one thing and one thing only. The almighty God, whose word is his work and whose work is his word and who is true and who is real.'

Oh, Christ on a bike, I think. She's going to start rolling her eyes back in her head any moment and speaking in tongues.

Has she got a fucking snake in that clutch-bag?

'I say to you, Mr. Vanikin, that you are a good man, the best here at Europa House. You have it within you to change this place, to do good works. I don't know if you are a religious man, Mr. Vanikin, and I don't care. Many work for the Lord who know him not. But I see a light coming from the clouds, and it shines with the glory of the word.'

If the old theatre curtains blacking out my windows parted and a host of archangels pulled up outside singing hosannahs at that precise moment — 3:47, by my new clock — I would say fair play to you. I sense a *dénouement*. Is she going to ask me to take over as pastor at the Church of the Divine Light, her, as it were, local? Reader, she is not. The sword of the Lord fell never heavier than her final words to me that day.

'Mr. Vanikin? You must found a SCHOOL!'

CHAPTER THIRTEEN

School for Vandals

Vanikin, Vanikin, all is Vanikin. At least, that seems to be the atmosphere at Europa House. What with Estrella's impassioned plea for me to continue what seem to be viewed as my good works, and now Mrs. Pallis urging me to institute some sort of missionary bunfight, it seems I am the man of the hour, hours which are ticking away, recorded by the pleasing *chock* of the ticking of my new clock.

A *school?* What on earth is the woman thinking? In here, for a start, the flat of Vanikin, essentially another small drawer in a large printer's casement, not only is there not room to swing a cat, there isn't room to have a bloody cat. No silk purse has yet been made whose provenance was a sow's ear.

Of course, I am — was — a teacher. But I was guiding students — even some willing ones — through the treacherous and serpentine backwaters of the dark continent of philosophy. I can't see me recommending *1-2-3 with Ant and Bee* as a set text with a call for essays, and that is the type of book many of the bustling and often criminal drones of Europa Hive would require as Life 101, as it were.

My musings are interrupted by the fairy-land trill of Estrella's knock at the door, her visits being as regular as Immanuel Kant's daily perambulation. Is it my imagination — fevered, at present, for reasons which should be obvious — or is the knock a little more urgent and purposeful than usual, which sounds like a dying dissident tapping out his final morse message on the wall of some Latin American prison cell? I admit the fluttering beazel herself, and she is, indeed, in a state which could only be described as heightened.

'Oh, Harry!'

I assume I am about to be regaled with yet another event from the well-stocked store-room of Estrella's *angst*. But what comes next merely serves to add additional capital to mine.

'Mrs. Pallis told me the news! Oh, well done, Harry! I'm so *proud* of you!'

'Well, it was only a CV, and we didn't lie all that much. In fact, I was wondering—'

'Not about Jimmy-Shawn, you goon. Well, a bit about Jimmy-Shawn, but only because he can go, too!'

'Go where?'

She looked at me as though I were a child in a behavioural unit wearing a bib and a rubber crash-hat.

'To your school!'

Oh, hammer in the nails, life, why don't you. Jab me in the side with your sword, and give me a vinegar poultice to go. You may as well. I came here, to the underworld, for a bit of peace and quiet, and what do I get? The love of the good people. Fortunately, I have my riposte ready, as previewed.

'Well, Estrella. I would love to, you know. But there are already schools, and, well—'

'Nonsense! The schools are hopeless. The children are more likely to learn how to put a condom on a banana than how to read!'

It isn't so much the accuracy of Estrella's social commentary that shocked me — she was sailing close to the line I took in *The Decadent Turn* — as the sexual overtones of her imagery. As a rule, Estrella may as well have gone around the place wearing a t-shirt reading: *I will grow old as a spinster.* I resort to Plan B.

'Look at this room. You and I practically mean anyone else will be standing room only.'

'Not here, you old goose!'

'Where, then?'

'In the games room, of course.'

Oh, Jesus, Mary, and Joseph. Dante writes, in private correspondence, that he had planned an eighth circle of hell for his great poem *L'Inverno*, but had omitted it from the final version of the work as he deemed it *too gruelling for the reader*. Well, reader, if there be such a circle, the games room at Europa House is surely that dread place. I have never visited that august establishment, obviously, but Lars the Danish lab technician's descriptions of it make it sound as though a Japanese slaughter in a Nanking opium den in 1940 would seem, by comparison, to be a tea-room scene at the Savoy. I counter again.

'Ah, but you see, Craig would never—'

'Do you know what Craig is doing now?'

Watching specialist pornography? Cooking methamphetamine sulphate? Child trafficking?

'Um, actually, no, I don't.'

'He's out doing Mrs. Podolski's shopping.'

If you got Sherlock Holmes, Miss Marple, Hercules Poirot, and Columbo together for a bridge four, I doubt whether they could find a reason for Craig McCerrow doing anything as remotely human as shopping for another person. My jaw is, as jaws will be on these occasions, agape.

'Why on earth would he be doing that?'

'I don't know. But he is. He has been doing lots of strange things since he talked to the measuring man.'

The measuring man has become 'the measuring man,' I note, taking on, as a name, the phrase which describes his function, like a town-cryer or a chimney-sweep. *Res, nomina*. By his measuring shall ye know him. I say,

'Well, I suppose we should be grateful.'

'Don't change the subject.'

'*I* didn't change the subject.'

'What will be your first lesson?'

'Estrella, look. I can't do it. I can't just start a school.'

'Oh, yes, you can.'

She's right, of course. I am in that awful, short period of time chess players experience when they look at the pieces and think: 'I'm buggered.' Of course, I could do it, except for the small consideration of the fact that I haven't left my monk's cell for over seven years. I think of the pit-horses in Zola's gruelling novel of the French mines, *Germinal.* Never seeing the sun, purblind, creatures of the shadows. We are interrupted by the knocketty-knock of our man in Denmark — or rather not in Denmark — with his news from nowhere. Estrella, despite her new authority and apparent forthrightness, will never stay when there is new company, but before she makes her hasty exit, I say,

'I will think it over. Can you come back later?'

'Yes. What time?'

She smiles, not an unbeguiling sight. She knows two things. One, Vanikin up until now set no store by clock-time. Two, Vanikin now has a clock. I say,

'Four of the clock.'

She smiles and leaves, Lars coming in as they pass awkwardly like a prisoner exchange, which, in a way, it is.

Estrella is not only up to something, she is drawing on reserves I didn't know she had, and, I suspect, neither did she. But I have a manoeuvre of my own device: Lars. I have specifically — albeit politely — instructed Lars to pre-edit the newspapers, like a conscientious *Pravda* sub-editor, so that I am told nothing about this city and, if at all possible, Britain as a whole. It is global oddities on which I thrive, and he has developed a refined sense of my tastes, like a brothel madame who keeps on seeing the same High Court judge and so knows what he likes. And so, I am beguiled for an hour by tales of Guatemalan carnivals found to be smuggling guns to what remains of Nicaragua's Sandinistas, ice hotels in Finnish Lapland, the return of Bubonic Plague in sub-Saharan Africa. It all melds into one, like the tales of a thousand and one nights told in an opium dream and in a pleasant Danish accent.

Lars bids his usual affable farewell, and I think about the strange times that have even begun to affect Europa House, which used to be able to pride itself on being strange. This place is a hothouse of psychological dysfunction. I should know; I am one of its prime exhibit orchids.

The world went mad a long time ago, in the same way that the nineteenth-century syphilitic went mad the moment the toxic little spirochaetes entered the brain. What we are seeing now — what I was seeing the last time I walked the overworld — is tertiary-stage syphilis, the last manic eruption of spittle and eye-rolling before death. Mankind was never meant to last, any more than the dodo or any other creature which was only issued a ticket, as with an airport car-park, for short-stay.

It's too late for teaching, past the hour where the transmission of the embers of knowledge could be fanned into the flames of wisdom, long gone bedtime for a drunk and absent humanity. All any of us can do is make peace with our makers and have one last drink in the next bar down from the last-chance saloon.

But I'm going to do it, anyway. Why? *Because* it's pointless. *Because* it's insane. *Because* it's *un poco loco*. In the end (times), the only sane response to an insane world is to out-crazy it. My school will be me spitting in the face of fate, curdling world-destiny's milk carton, telling the universe it can *fuck off.*

I wind the clock. It is the hour when first I wound it, excitedly, and vowed I would wind it at that time every day until there was no more Vanikin, no more time, no more need to insert the heavy, square-slotted key into the hole on the front and make the few resistant twists to keep the old ticker going, my old ticker, anyone's old ticker. The caretaker. The measuring-man. The clock-winder. Our functions will adorn our gravestones. Comes Estrella's knock on the door, scarcely recognisable, like a full-grown bounding hare grown from a timid blinking leveret.

And through the door comes a changed Estrella, entering into yet another alteration, like a pupa approaching the time to become a butterfly. I've got you now. She sits with a new confidence, lady rather than stuttering, twitching wight. I prepare one of her anti-infusions and myself a cup of the good stuff, beloved of builders and plumbers the country wide and long. To battle. She says,

'You wanted to see me.'

'Yes, I did, didn't I.'

'I know it's hard, Harry, but think of all the good it would do. Not just Jimmy-Shawn. Marek. Declan. Suze. Adam. Bertie Spedding. And you could have an adult class; Mrs. Schumpeter, Mr. Pilkington, Mrs. Podolski. Teach them about, I don't know, the Greeks or something. Oh, *think* of what you could do!'

'I have been thinking.'

'And?'

'And I'm going to do it.'

'Oh, Harry!'

And she springs up like a gazelle, throwing her slender arms around my scrawny old turkey's neck for a most unprecedented and unheard-of hug. The feeling of human warmth, so long a foreign land to the exiled Vanikin. We are in strange times. I continue, moving cobra-like for the take.

'There's one condition.'

'Yes!'

'I am going to need a teaching assistant.'

'Perfect! Sarah! My friend Sarah. She actually *is* a teaching assistant; that's what she does. She—'

'It's okay. I know a perfect assistant.'

'Oh. Great. Who?'

'You.'

'Oh, now, Harry. I couldn't. I mean, I just couldn't; I can't.'

'Then neither can I. It's the only condition, but it is what I believe they call on television a deal-breaker.'

And she looks a rueful look, sees the options, and says, after an internal struggle I would have liked to have seen represented by a neuropathological cross-section of her brain,

'Okay. Okay!'

'Good. Then we need to have a pre-school meeting.'

'Tomorrow, usual time?'

'Tomorrow is fine. What is the usual time? So I can inform the clock.'

She smiles again. This is becoming a regular laugh-in.

'Ten.'

'Perfect. Oh, and have you got a computer?'

'You muffin. Of *course*, I've got a computer. You are about the only person in the world who hasn't got a computer. Mrs. Schumpeter even has a computer. She's got email and everything.'

'Jimmy-Shawn's CV. I want you to type it out and print it.'

I hand her my hand-written hoax on the world of UK employment.

'Okay. I'll bring it tomorrow.'

'You're forgetting one thing.'

'What's that?'

'For the last seven years and a bit — see my sister if you

want it to the hour — I haven't been out of this room.'

She looks at me, a new and serious look I haven't seen before. She says,

'Yes, you have.'

I look back, equally grave.

She was right. Yes, I had.

CHAPTER FOURTEEN

Measure for Measure

I had been outside. It was in the fourth year of my self-imposed exile here among the shades, and it was the fault of that most unreliable of shadows which was to blame, the one Plato — as noted in a previous instalment — calls 'a shadow which keeps us company.' The body.

By that time, I was snugly at home at Europa House. Most of the cast who make up the tragi-comedy of my life were already assembled, and I knew that, no matter how much time I had left to me, I would die here. I had my books, a food-and-goods delivery service in the form of the boy, and the company of the decent and the indecent. All human life was here. Why not join the fun?

So, what, you may enquire, was the reason for my short excursion into the vacuous horror of the outside world? What bloom did Vanikin feel was unplucked, which sunset unseen or vista unviewed? None of the above. It was for a reason linked inextricably with what the inestimable *Oxford English Dictionary* — that marvellous book which merely requires its component words to be placed in the right order to give the long-sought answer to the meaning of life — defines as something 'small and having no known function.' How appropriate, in these end times.

My fucking appendix burst.

I had noticed something amiss in the Vanikin interior

plumbing system in the days leading up to my hospitalisation. Not being a medical man, and with the added impediments of being male, and thus less likely to visit a doctor than the more watchful female of the species, and my determination to live in the desert and apart from the ways of men — and women, for that matter — I soldiered on, staggering occasionally and woken by a terrible griping python running amok in the nether regions. One day, after opening the door on my knees to a horrified Estrella, she recognised this not as some gesture of supplication, but the symptom of an awful dysfunction. She called an ambulance.

I really don't remember much about the next three days. I was bounced down the stairs — my stretcher wouldn't fit in the *ad hoc* mobile urinal which poses as a lift — by a West Indian and a Pole who were perfectly pleasant and encouraging. I think I slept in the ambulance. I recall being lectured by a stern Ghanaian nurse in Accident & Emergency for not coming in sooner. Then, I remember coming round in a ward full of mostly young men, all of whom seemed to have been in motor-car or motorcycle accidents. The whole thing was very horrible, and my sister and Estrella are to be awarded the highest honours for their role in Vanikin's brush with death. A burst appendix is not as bad as, say, a burst condom full of heroin in one's lower intestine at the Colombian border, but it is, by all accounts, a question of degree on the same scale.

Anyway, when I was back in my reliable old bed at Europa House, tended by Estrella and Mrs. Podolski, to whom I gave a key so that they could get copies cut, I was made to promise to go to a doctor if anything like that should happen again. I promised, like a good but rather naughty boy. I have ever since prayed to the indefinite deity I feel has some say over my fate that this ricketty, clinking and clanking, wheezing and sneezing old bag of bones won't act the giddy goat ever again, because I never, ever want to go out into the world again. Images, flashbacks, scenes from a dream.

Looking down from my stretcher outside Europa House and seeing a pile of dogshit so large it could never have been produced by any canine breed known to man, crouching malevolently, angrily uncleaned-up, just sitting there like a family Christmas pudding. A man in the hospital waiting room who appeared to be a giant robot lizard — and this before the administration of what were rather agreeable drugs — with his head bald, save for two scarlet tufts like devil's horns, and sporting earlobes that resembled those of an African tribesman and seemed to contain small ice-hockey pucks, like casino chips. Metal spikes protruded from his lips, nose, and eyebrows. A white nurse with a port-wine stain on her neck the exact shape of Belgium, who I would see again as I entered the underworld. Hospital porters coming to the ward in the middle of the night to a bed surrounded by a screen. They were wearing white overalls and masks. They took the man away, covered in a sheet. The man in the end bed, two away from the dead man, being gently and efficiently masturbated by his girlfriend or wife or, at the very least, a woman of his acquaintance.

Gah! Even the thought of what is out there frightens me, the fact that everyone else, everywhere and all around, have this and scenes like it as the grist of their daily experience. What went wrong with the world, and when? The expulsion from Eden? The demise of the dinosaur? The Industrial Revolution? Last Thursday? What time, exactly? Time.

It is 9:45 a.m., and there is a knock at the door, Estrella's new, improved knock, now with added missionary zeal. If nothing else, if this school was a Light-Brigade charge in entirely the wrong direction, at the very least, Estrella has seen what she is and could become. I go to the door with a light, tripping step, practically Nijinsky as I arrive at the door and open it to greet my teaching assistant.

But it is not Estrella.

It is a man, inexpensively suited and tieless, and he is carrying a tape measure. He says,

'Mr. Vanikin?'

'Yes?'

'Might I come in and take some measurements?'

Yes, well, that is pretty much what science said to philosophy in the eighteenth century, and we all know how that turned out.

'Um, well, I—'

'Sorry. You'll want to see some identification. I'm from the local authority.'

He produces a laminated ID like a stage conjurer producing the missing ace — not, one would hope, the deadly ace of spades. The photograph is certainly him, a slightly plump, rather amiable face. He could have been a pastor, perhaps, in a Bavarian village of the early seventeenth century, wary of being caught reading Luther, but secretly doing so anyway once the cows were milked and prayers all said and done. I say,

'Do come in.'

And so it is that, for the next half hour, Mr. Roger Perrett measures Vanikin's cell while the old clock squats on the table measuring time. The day of measuring has begun. While Roger measures, we talk easily. I say,

'Can I ask you what the measurements are for?'

He takes down his calibrations in rather a stylish little calico notebook, not the spiral-bound, four-for-a-quid *tabula rasa* one might expect.

'Certainly! We at the department have been led to believe that the residents here are being asked to pay rent for accommodation which, quite frankly, is not up to scratch.'

'Not big enough?'

'Not big enough. Among other things.'

Convincing enough. I noted that he hadn't given me the name of the department, meaning that any attempt to check his *bona fides* would lead to the novel Franz Kafka never got around to writing. Local authorities — Estrella's silly name for what I call the council — are like the maze of Daedalus, but with no Ariadne and her useful ball of twine on hand. I say,

'But you can't make any of the flats larger. Space is space.'

I am aware of the conflict between Newtonian and Leibnizian space, obviously, but that is not really my point, and I don't bring it up. After my recent musings on time, it was pleasant to flip the disc over and play the Kantian B-side, space.

'No, but we can get the rent lowered. And a few other services wouldn't be a bad thing. Although that's not my department.'

I was becoming interested in this new arrival, this calibratory *arriviste*. Was he what he claimed to be, or a wolf in cheap clothing? He was now measuring the floor in my main 'room', and I thought of being jocular, suggesting, perhaps, that it would be nice to have the extra space should I need to host an evening of quadrilles and *baccarat*. Hush, Vanikin. Your attempts at humour are not needed here. I say,

'Do you have the power to change private sector rent?'

'We can enforce the Fair Rent Act.'

'So. The landlord is not operating in the private sector, in the true sense of the word.'

'Well, if he was, you would have it a lot worse. There are checks and balances.'

There. Now I have it. There is something unnatural about the way he is responding to my questions. Not only is he too intelligent to be a council worker measuring rabbit-hutches for a living, but he is unfazed by *my* apparent intelligence and acuity. Did he get this line of questioning from Declan, for example, or did that Irish rogue merely ask if he wanted to buy any drugs?

'Well, that's you done, Mr. Vanikin. It is Mr., I take it? You're not a doctor or anything?'

'Actually, I'm a professor.'

'Are you, indeed? Well, well.'

'Retired.'

'And can I ask in which subject?'

'Ask away. Philosophy.'

'Good lord! I think we read some Plato at school. I couldn't make head nor tail of it, Mr. Vanikin. Professor Vanikin.'

'Please. Call me Harry.'

'Right. Well, Harry, as I say, you're all done.'

'You can say that again.'

And he laughed, naturally, I thought. He really was a riddle wrapped in a conundrum wrapped in a Marks & Spencer suit.

'No, Harry. You seem as fit as a fiddle to me. And as bright as a button. That's funny. Those are things my mother used to say.'

'Is your mother still alive?'

'No. Cancer. Four years ago.'

'Well, Roger — if I may call you Roger — you have helped to keep her alive, in a small way.'

He looked at me quizzically, then said,

'Harry, I think you are one of the most interesting people I've ever met. Goodbye. For now.'

'Goodbye. And thank you. For, well, your measuring.'

'I always like to take sensible measures. Sorry. I always use that joke.'

'Is it yours?'

'Yes. As far as I know.'

'Well, I think it's funny.'

And Roger Perrett, our man of the measure, takes his leave.

Almost immediately, the knock I am expecting arrives. This

time, I use my door-cracking ruse to ensure that it is, indeed, my new teaching assistant, and it transpires that it is. Estrella breezes in with a smile and a hello, but still a trace of that old haunted look. She sits and says,

'What was he doing here?'

'Measuring. He is the measuring man, is he not?'

'Well, hasn't measured my flat!'

'Which is number sixty-four. Mine is number thirty-nine. Can you see an indicator? Maybe I need a new teaching assistant already. Why have you got an easel and a sketch-pad? I cannot take an art class.'

'We're going to plan our first lesson! This is *so exciting!*'

What have I done? Well, for the time being, I have changed someone's life. For the better. Can this be a bad thing? And she isn't wearing her usual drab's weeds, cardigan and wartime skirt, but a white cotton shirt and jeans and boots. She sets up her easel and shuffles it into a space where it sort of fits.

'Now! Craig is fine about the games room. We organise our first lesson, and then, we set a date.'

Time, always time.

CHAPTER FIFTEEN

The Follies of Pygmalion

I know what you're thinking. I see all. I didn't read the greatest minds of men for all those years not to be able to look into the minds of the meanest. I see the cogs whirring, the levers and springs clicking, the ratchets and the motors and the gears. I see all, and I know what you're thinking, and you should hang your head in shame.

What you are thinking runs as follows. Look at him, that old deep-sea fossil Vanikin, curled and ribbed like the ghost of some forsaken, long-dead trilobite, preening his sparse and tatty, ground-dragging feathers for some sleek bird just over a third of his age, trying, with what's left of all his might, to impress a young woman.

You should be ashamed of yourselves.

And yet, and yet…

Philosophy gifts the long-term resident in its house a Janus-faced gift, the potlach of auto-gnosis, of knowing oneself in stretched-out obedience to the Delphic oracle, boarded up and unrentable as it now is. Vanikin knows many things, and one of them is that he knows nothing. Could it be? Am I so far gone in my miserable and forlorn dotage that I can't see that I am simply trying to impress the girls, a girl?

Oh, it's monstrous, absurd, a grotesquerie in a world of grotesques. Could it be that I harbour dark and inappropriate feelings for Estrella? Inappropriate teaching methods.

Inappropriate leching methods. Or is it, as I suspect and hope, a desire to build, and to build well?

You may recall the tale of Pygmalion and Galatea. The Greek myths, with their constant round of metamorphoses and rogering, contain all of life's oddities, like a carney side-show, and it is to talk of sculpture and the sculptor that I have gathered you here today.

Pygmalion, son of Belus, was a sculptor, and when it came to the ladies, he set his sights high and fell in love with Aphrodite, no less. She, however, was not the kind of goddess to hang around with any old sculptor, and gave him what I believe our transatlantic cousins term the bum's rush. Out of sorts, miffed, and with his nose like Hamlet's version of time, out of joint, Pygmalion activated plan B, which was to make an ivory statue of Aphrodite and put his case to her. He also slept with her — sex dolls not having been invented then, even by the forge of Hephaestus — and soon, she did what things are always doing in the Greek myths. She came to life, and Pygmalion named her Galatea.

That inveterate and extravagantly bearded old fraud George Bernard Shaw, who never saw a fascist dictator he didn't like, immortalised the myth in his play *Pygmalion*, which was, in turn, adapted for the big screen as *My Fair Lady*, starring the rogueish Rex Harrison and elfin beauty Audrey Hepburn, and so has, to a certain extent, sunk in to our modern *mythos* in addition to its Greek origins. Has it now made one further frog-jump to the fresh lily-pad of Europa House? Do my statue's previously cold and marble veins now run quick with warm life?

Pah! Enough of this paltry nonsense, Vanikin. To the matter in hand.

Estrella, whether or not she is a creation of the Vanikin hammer and chisel, is an organised taskmistress, everything a teaching assistant should be, in my experience, and she deals with my questions, objections, and general cavils with the ease of a professional tennis player swatting back the feeble lobs of a chip-fattened office worker. What of, I say, the disparity among the potential students, of whom, incidentally, there look like being quite a few? For example, Declan can't read, not even his own name, while Mrs. Podolski likes nothing better than to curl up with her cat, a cup of tea, and Pushkin. Estrella replies,

'Simple. We have an introductory lesson. We can't show up people who can't read or write or do arithmetic, so we have to have separate classes. Like any school. Remedial writing will be one of them.'

'I've never taught that. Mind you, a lot of my students would be all thumbs with a betting slip.'

'My friend Sarah will tell me all about it. I'm having lunch with her.'

Again, Galatea speaks. In the seven plus years I have known her, I have never heard Estrella talk of any social life whatsoever outside of the black hole and event horizon of Europa House. I continue my objections to the bench.

'What about the council?'

'Local authority. What about them?'

'If they find out we are running a school here, they will close it down.'

'How will they find out?'

I felt like a backgammon player seeing a winning dash of all his little discs hoving into view.

'You are forgetting Roger Perrett, he who men call the measuring man.'

'But you're his friend.'

'And how have you leapt to *that* conclusion?'

'I saw his face when he left your flat. He looked as a happy as Larry.'

'Who is Larry?'

'My dad used to say it.'

Again, new curves and details emerge on the statue's surface. Estrella is clearly becoming an amateur psychologist. Also, I have never, even once, heard her refer to either of her parents. In my experience, if people do not mention the sire and the dam, there is a reason for that. I say,

'Well, we had a chat.'

'Besides, it hasn't got anything to do with him. It's not—'

'His department. I know. But what about Craig? He isn't going to let anything happen which he can't control or interfere with or sell drugs to anyone or everyone involved.'

'Craig is gardening.'

'He's *what*?'

'He's doing the garden. He's been given money to buy rose bushes. Mrs. Pallis told him to go and buy them. He's planting them now.'

A mad world, my masters. I was running out of avoidance tactics. I say,

'Right. Well. When are we going to start?'

'Next week. I have to arrange chairs and a whiteboard.'

'Not a blackboard?'

'No, not a blackboard. A whiteboard. With a magic marker and a wipe cloth. Oh! I mustn't forget to buy those.'

'Are you spending money on this, Estrella?'

'I do have some money, you know. Well, a little bit.'

So, we work up the framework of a first lesson, my assistant and I — all we need is an actual subject... — and she goes on her way. I lunch on a fine tin of ravioli and bread and butter, with a can of mandarin slices and evaporated milk to follow, waving away the cheese-board, brandy, and Havana. I'm not always in the mood. And I sit on my throne — I sit there more now than on the ex-sofa, and I am not blind to the regal significance — with my feet on the second guest chair and think about teaching.

Teachers in Africa — not that I've ever been — are revered, worshipped by the tribe, who realise, somewhere in the tangle of myth, magic, and manhood, that the reason the white man is where he is and they are where they are is to do with knowledge. And knowledge, as Plato was among the first to inform a waiting world, requires transmission from one who has more of it to one who does not have so much. It is the only re-distribution of wealth that ever really worked. *Mwalimu.* 'Teacher' in Swahili. *Mwalimu* Vanikin *Tuan.* There he is, in his crumpled linen suit, cheroot lit and smoldering, fanned by a great palm leaf, Vanikin teaching Shakespeare to coolie village runners.

I enjoyed my time teaching in that I enjoyed the company of students. It reminded me of my own relatively happy years as an undergraduate, before life got its hooks in me and suspended me in mid-air before dropping me through a trapdoor that led all the way to Europa House. With philosophy, of course, there were students who were all frowns and furrowed brows from the off. 'But why prove the table is there?' they would say with an air of Archimedean triumph. 'My coffee cup is sitting on it. If it wasn't there, the cup would drop and break.' Ah, but would it, though? Hume would say that you may have seen that happen, but that is no guarantee of its happening on every occasion in the future. You see cups and tables. You never, ever see cause and effect. 'Why, one student asked exasperatedly, 'would I *want* to prove the table is there?' Now she was closer to the truth than some of the others who could see the point of the proof and its corollary. Philosophy.

Whatever happened to philosophy? You know, nice kid, always asking questions, smart kid. Used to hang out with the sciences. I think she was the hand-maiden to theology for a while back in the day. Now? Still hangs around the universities, you know. Trying to find work, like a stevedore on the docks.

Philosophy's had a bit of a fall from grace. There used to be a bit of respect. They shut Galileo and Descartes up for philosophising, nicked Boethius, poisoned Socrates, and *burnt* Bruno and Wycliff and Jan Huss. Now, a tenured departmental philosopher has no real incentive to crane his head above the trenches, although a new set of beliefs still threaten the unwary academic.

When it became increasingly apparent, post-Enlightenment, that most of what philosophy was doing was actually fledgling science, the resulting schism, had it been framed in the terms of a modern divorce, meant that science got the kids, the house, the car, and the pension. Philosophy was left with some old cardboard boxes filled with the stuff science had no use for, morality, metaphysics, and language, as well as some post-Romantic pop-psychology which coalesced into existentialism. That and a broken guitar and some CDs with cracked cases. From there, it was just some pyrotechnics and a little snake oil, and we got the three-ring circus of structuralism, post-structuralism, and post-modernism. These were like having the bad hangover without the pleasure of getting drunk first. Teaching stopped being so much fun then when, as Plato warned, the teachers started trying to impress the students.

That is when it arrived, the Pythagoras moment, the Einstein moment, the Socratic turn. I wasn't just going to teach reading and writing, history, English, maths. I was going to teach wisdom. I may not have been the world's most successful or happiest human being, but I could show others the way, like those tennis coaches who got knocked out in the first round of Wimbledon every year but used their understanding of technique to show others how to make it all the way to the final.

I see that Estrella is not the only one who has changed.

Two months ago — a block of time I see as a sort of unrolled tarpaulin — I would have been thinking of nothing more than whether Schopenhauer's pessimism in *The World as Will and Idea* was inextricably linked to what a grumpy old sod the man himself was in his life, or whether to have tinned pears or cling peaches for dessert. Now, I am suddenly striding purposefully across the Athenian square to enlighten the populace, bring light where there is darkness, and generally act like *Mwalimu* Vanikin *Tuan*. At least, I hope I am. There remains a dragon to slay, a ghost to placate, and an internal mutiny to be put down, a nagging, jeering, prancing goblin that will not stop pulling on the hem of my jester's silks. And it involves an action which, as detailed, I have performed but once in seven years, and that not of my own free will, that old matron.

I have to go outside.

CHAPTER SIXTEEN

In the Antechamber

Waking to a quiet underworld, noiseless save for the hum of Europa House itself, the life of any building, its cloudy marrow coursing round its rusty old veins, Vanikin dons his ceremonial garb, ye dressing-gowne of solitude, and sits mulling over one of Seneca's invaluable letters to his friend Lucilius. By Christ, Seneca kept those Roman postmen busy. Writing on the value of retirement, and referring to one of Lucilius' muckers and oppos, presumably, the wise and fated old Senator has this to say:

> *Encourage your friend to despise stout-heartedly those who upbraid him because he has sought the shade of retirement and has abdicated his career of honours, and, though he might have attained more, has preferred tranquillity to them all.*

Shade of retirement, yes. Did I abdicate my career of honours? Not in that I was forced from my place in the pantheon, no. The university, after the absurd stink that arose from the apparent unmasking of the 'far-Right tract' — a reviewer really did call *The Decadent Turn* that — made it reasonably clear to me that they would rather cause an old man distress than anger the young people, who now run universities with a dogmatic zeal that would have impressed the ecclesiastical authorities of the fifteenth century. As for tranquillity, I am alone with my books, like Faustus, and I have built for myself a sort of separate peace.

And now, I am seeking to withdraw the mandate of heaven from precisely that haven of words in which I nestle, like a little woodland creature burrowing down among the leaves and the loam. I thought I had made my circle in the world. Now it appears that there is an unfinished arc. If I am Prospero in his cell, I should know that the conjurer's circle cannot remain incomplete. That is how the devils get in.

I breakfast on porridge, the staple diet of the disenfranchised, and make a cup of tea in accompaniment. I think of Conrad, that old sea-dog and gambler, with his pointy beard and his well-cut suits, and his description, in *An Outcast of the Islands*, of the natural solitude each one of us is and has:

> *[T]he tremendous fact of our isolation, of the loneliness impenetrable and transparent, elusive and everlasting; of the indestructible loneliness that surrounds, envelopes, clothes every human soul from the cradle to the grave, and, perhaps, beyond.*

Now Vanikin, more grave than cradle, can't see beyond his next slice of toast and too-sweet, corner-shop marmalade. I'm not afraid of going out into the outside world. To listen to the prim and politically correct martinet who cast me from my academic Eden, you would have thought the outside world had more to fear from me. There are new gods now, new scriptures and new preachers. And, like all the conquered territories of religious doctrine, they require heretics to maintain their momentum. What is the point of belief if you can't punish someone for not believing? I had noticed it, incrementally and in an accretional drip-drip-drip of orthodoxy, with each year's fresh input of philosophy undergraduates who, far from being the screaming mob-in-waiting attendant on the social sciences, that waster of academic time, were still clear — the white ones, anyway — that they were no longer able to consider themselves in any way the solutions to the world's problems, having been told since they were small that they were the problem.

Now that I am seriously considering taking on students again, what is waiting for me? Of course, as mentioned, I won't be discussing Plato's *Theaetetus* with Jimmy-Shawn Pallis, but here, we will find raw material quite probably untainted by the wearisome mores of these interesting times. What is happening to me? Is the teaching impulse some long-dead need brought back to life, some *revenant* to be called from the depths to serve its master? Yes, or to find a new servant. We teach ourselves to teach others, as my favourite teacher once said. The door bursts into life with a fusillade of knocks, and I open it gingerly, that gateway through which Vanikin will soon pass once more not, this time and one hopes, on his knees and clutching his wounded side like a stricken hoplite at Thermopylae. Oh, Crivens. It is the errant force of nature known to mortals as Declan.

'Mr. V.! Okay if I come in?'

'Yes, Declan. Come in.'

Declan enters, as always, as though he is a student of ecclesiastical architecture walking cautiously and investigatively into a new-found priest-hole in a stately home. He sits in my guest chair as though it were an electric one. I say,

'And how are you?'

'Oh, you know, Mr. V. Usual cheeky chappie. Paddy abroad.'

'Are you actually from Ireland, Declan?'

'Ah yeah. Fock yeah! Galway. Roses and beautiful women and Guinness.'

'Do they not have those all over the Emerald Isle?'

'S'pose they do. Not as good as Galway, dough. Estrella says youse is starting a school.'

Well, I suppose advertising is the modern way of spreading

knowledge. It suddenly occurs to me that anyone at Europa House may be coming along to my new Christchurch College, even if only out of curiosity.

'We are, indeed.'

'Estrella looks great! What did you do?'

'How do you mean?'

'Well, you see, she usually walks round like she's at a funeral, or *goin'* to a funeral, or *comin' back* from a funeral. Now, she looks great!'

Strange that Declan needs to cover all the possible temporal relations between a funeral mourner and their attendant funeral, but I suppose thoroughness is to be admired in the young.

'Would you like some tea?'

'Ah, no sure Mr. V. It's nice of you, dough. I'm going to The Leather Pig for a few with me brother Kooks.'

'Kooks?'

'Yeah. Bet you thought we 'as all called Paddy, dincha, Mr. V.?'

'No, but I suppose "Kooks" is a nickname.'

'Short For Cúchullain.'

'Cúchullain?'

'He was an Irish hero, loik. In the olden days. The real olden days, loik, waaay before the First World War an dat.'

'He certainly was a hero. He defended Ulster and saved the Brown Bull from Queen Medb's army.'

'Fockin. Hell. How did you know that?'

He slaps himself in the head like a cartoon character.

'I forgot! You're the biggest brainbox in...the jungle. What's it like knowing everything?'

'Well, I don't know everything, Declan.'

'You know a fockin' shite lot, dough, Mr. V. Thing is, can Kooks come?'

'Can he come where?'

'To the school, loik.'

'Well, it was supposed to be for the House only.'

'Ah, *please*. It'll just be him. I'll not be bringing Rory and Connelly and Rosie Porter and dem conts. Oops, sorry. Language.'

'Well, yes, he can.'

'Ah, thanks, Mr. V. You're the best teacher ever. Better than the shoites at my school. Kooks is going to be fockin' dismal that you know what his name means!'

And Declan takes his leave for his next appointment, leaving me to ponder his use of the word 'dismal'. That, as Proust wrote, is what the young people say, I suppose. Words lose their meaning, along with everything else, casually strolling across the semantic floor to take up residence among the antonyms. Is this Nietzsche's transvaluation of all values, only wearing training shoes in place of stout Bavarian walking boots?

Don't let them, Vanikin! This is what the voice is saying, the voice of the inner Vanikin you knew was there, like a trapdoor hidden beneath a rug all these years that opens onto a steep staircase that leads down to a dim cellar that winds beneath the world and leads to a door that hides the way back to the light and the room and the undisturbed rug. The voice of your favourite teacher, the voice of the centuries, the voice of the Lady Philosophy in the cell of Boethius, the voice of old Socrates in the Athenian square. They tried Socrates on the charge of corrupting youth, but he wasn't corrupting anyone but those who thought they knew what was what when they spoke.

I sit in my chair and grip the arms like an astronaut experiencing the blast moonward, like a teenager in a fairground ride, waiting for the dipping and rolling to start, the screams of the other teenagers around me as the world turns upside-down and rightways up again. Philosophy. Seneca, again:

> *Betake yourself therefore to philosophy if you would be safe, untroubled, happy, in fine, if you wish to be free.*

Free. I thought I was doing a Hamlet in a nutshell and crowning myself king of infinite space, but, in the end, four walls — even Gyproc ones — *do* a prison make. And if Estrella is Ariadne — not that you could exactly get lost in this place, twine or no twine — then perhaps I must be led out to meet my destiny.

A knock, always the knock. I open the door and see the stately figure of Mrs. Podolski, reader of Russian literature and one-time seamstress to the aristocracy. I bid her come in.

'Mrs. Podolski. How nice. Cup of tea?'

Perhaps I should explain that I have no gilded samovar, merely a mug, a wounded kettle, and some tea-bags.

'No, thank you, Mr. Vanikin.'

'Please, sit down.'

Mrs. Podolski gathers herself like a hanging judge with an itch.

'Mr. Vanikin. I want to say to you that I think you are doing something which is a good thing.'

Mrs. Podolski, it strikes me, would have made an excellent logical positivist. Clarity of expression is never to be sniffed or sneered at, and here is a sentence of which Tarski would have been proud.

'Well, I hope so.'

'To learn is of the most importance, to the old — like us, Mr. Vanikin — as much as to the young. But to learn requires one who teaches.'

I wish I were writing this all down, but etiquette frowns on notetaking during social interaction.

'Yes, I am not sure exactly *what* I will be teaching to begin with. But little steps first.'

'Yes, and yes! The giant stride cannot be made from the standing position.'

If nothing else, Mrs. Podolski has a glittering career ahead of her writing fortune-cookie aphorisms for the better class of Chinese restaurant. I say,

'Will you be attending?'

'For all the world, I would not miss this! I wanted only to say one thing, and it is friendly advice alone.'

'Certainly. Please do.'

'To bring the people of Europa House together, teach at first something about which they all know.'

Are we on the grounds of the Platonic *sensus communis*? By Jove, I believe we are!

'I will bear that very much in mind. Thank you, Mrs. Podolski.'

'And now, I must take my leave. Lars, who is such a gentleman, is bringing me the newspaper.'

'And will be reading it to me later, I hope. If we have the stomach for it.'

'Ha ha ha! Oh, surely. The world outside these walls is a strange one, Mr. Vanikin! So! I bid you a good and productive day.'

And Mrs. Podolski is gone, in a train of wisdom and Delphic injunction. I sit back and give my tea a tentative slurp. This good lady is on to something, but what? Something that is common to all the inhabitants of Europa House? A tough call, as the young people say. What unites Lars, Declan, Marvin M., Estrella, Craig, and Mrs. Podolski? Air, and the necessity of breathing it. I am struggling already to expand the list. What common element, what shared experience can serve as a stanchion or foundation-stone to unite these disparate elements in the social periodic table? What on God's good and green earth do they have in common, these shades of one dwelling, these livers and movers and havers of their being, in the shadows of Europa House?

Then, it came, fell into my lap like Newton's famous apple, the one which undid the harm wrought by the apple eaten in Eden. One common point of reference for the residents of Europa House? Easy.

Europa House.

Chapter Seventeen
Europa After the Rain

The original plans for Europa House were drawn up by the London County Council's Architect's Department in 1960. I imagine pipe-smoking men frowning over huge sheets of paper, one pointing here or there, making a point about light orientation and the setting of the sun, the others nodding in agreement or frowning with sceptical expressions, thoroughly classical men assessing the movement of the classical Phobos and his chariot, its motions and course. Nowadays, they will have been replaced by charmless accountants in training shoes using Lego.

The original four-block design contained eighty-three apartments arranged around a central double courtyard, and, although this was later extended, it still forms the core of the project. In the intervening period, the original apartments were gutted and sub-divided when it was discovered that, no matter what Stakhanovite efforts go into uglifying a city, people must still live there, hemmed in by the geographical location of the agents of commerce. If you build it, they may not necessarily want to come, but they will. And then, they can't leave.

The estate's postcode places it just within the Bermondsey and Southwark ward of London, and it is hard by the River Thames. Charles Dickens set part of his novel *Oliver Twist* nearby, and old Fagin's school for thievery was situated in or around rooms above one of the old mills. Old Fagin and old

Vanikin, partners in crime after all these years. Bill Sykes swung his final swing in this world from a dockside wharf not a catapult shot's distance from where I write.

During World War II, due to its proximity to major docks such as Rotherhithe and factories in Bermondsey, Herman Göring's Luftwaffe marked the area out for special attention, killing four hundred civilians in the process, and leaving various unexploded ordinance in its wake. I well remember the terrifying day two years ago, sitting waiting for Estrella to arrive to tell me whether we were all going to be evacuated due to an unexploded bomb found a few hundred yards from Europa House. As it was, Hitler failed posthumously to force Vanikin, a veteran agoraphobic of Russian provenance, to move house yet again. An apocryphal tale exemplifying the British 'Blitz spirit' concerns an old lady emerging from a lone Anderson shelter — these were concrete bunkers used to protect families from the bombing — covered in dust, and shouting to her friend inside,

'There you are, Emily. I told you it was a bomb.'

At the turn of the twentieth century, the area was predominantly home to the working class, as opposed to Europa House's current status as predominantly home to the non-working class. Being a self-contained area whose hub was the rapidly expanding docks, workers tended to be housed there, as one would expect, and this made the area less of a suburb and more of a township. To quote Milton — somewhat out of context, as he was writing about the period after the English Civil War — from his *The History of Britain: Especially that part now called England*:

> *Everyone betooke himself...to doe as his own profit or ambition ledd him'. And it led many skilled watermen, lightermen, and stevedores to do just that, along with the*

concomitant tanners, millers, and ostlers attendant on the
incoming goods from an expanding empire.

In the nineteenth century, the area was home to London's first railway in 1836, its first viaduct in 1866, and the Tower subway in 1869. Guy's Hospital was opened nearby in the preceding century, by Thomas Guy in 1721. Like everywhere else, the area which would go on to produce Europa House was a marshy pond of primeval slime, which, over the centuries, spawned Cluniac monasteries — torn down by Henry VIII as part of his thorough-going wedding preparations — abbeys, theatres, schools, and slums as the riverside area was reclaimed from its natural marshland state. Queen Elizabeth I, the Faerie Queene herself, once visited Sir Thomas Pope just around the corner from Europa House. What would she make of her subjects now?

From the egg of Mrs. Podolski's idea to the hatchling — in more ways than one — of Estrella's research efforts via the vast information deserts of the internet, to Vanikin's summation and upcoming presentation, we have all the makings of a first lesson. Estrella has also done a fine job on Jimmy-Shawn Pallis' CV, presenting it to me in a plastic wallet with its own covering sheet at which Jimmy-Shawn gazed as though it were the Dead Sea scrolls.

The document itself may contain as close a relation to real-world events as the Celestine Prophecies, but if it helps Jimmy-Shawn get on in this treacherous world, full to brimming, as it already is, with deception and lies, then I am happy to have played the role of well-meaning deceiver, Puckish, Robin Goodfellow. I have also offered to stand as a reference for Jimmy-Shawn in my professorial capacity. How could I do other, when not to do so may be to condemn him to a life of powerful cannabis, street crime, and gold dentistry?

First, though, there is an initiation ceremony to be

undergone, a *rite de passage* for old Vanikin, scarcely less daunting than the initiation of the chosen adept into the frightening Eleusinian mysteries of the Greeks, although, thankfully, not requiring the wearing either of a toga or a circlet of laurel leaves on the wrinkled old brow. Here, the lightly and jauntily tapped door tells me, is my guide.

Estrella says nothing, her smile increasingly doing her talking for her. She is carrying a walking-stick with a *faux* ivory handle carved into the shape of an eagle, and one of those rubber butts on the end to prevent slippage. She says,

'I found it in the charity shop when I bought your clock.'

'Are you ill?'

'It's for you, Harry. You haven't walked anywhere for seven years.'

'I walk to the toilet.'

'Harry!'

'Alright, alright. But you may as well get me a hearing-trumpet and a tartan blanket to put across my knees, so I don't catch cold.'

'Shall we have a cup of tea first?'

'Right-ho. Which of your, um, teas would you like?'

'Let me have a look at all of them, so I can choose.'

'Right-ho.'

Vanikin, scared and vulnerable, a little boy in the sea again, waves up to his chest, voice just a little too cheerful. I root out all the dreadful concoctions Estrella favours and put them in my useful basket, a small wicker affair I keep for just this type of commission, rare as it is. Thrifty, practical Vanikin. I give the basket to Estrella, and she goes through the contents, smiling occasionally. Then, she passes the basket back to me and says,

'Thought so. It's all crap really, isn't it? None of them taste of anything. Throw them in the bin and make me a cup of builder's tea will you, Harry?'

And Galatea smiles again, a breezy, unaffected smile. She doesn't twitch any more, her eyes look straight at me and don't dart around as though she were trying to monitor the progress of many dragon-flies. I prepare tea and say,

'Where are we going, exactly?'

'Oh, just round to the courtyard today. We'll go a bit further tomorrow.'

'Tomorrow?'

'Harry. This isn't a once-in-a-lifetime visit to London to see the changing of the guard. I read psychological articles about people who haven't been out for a long time. They can't just go straight to Brighton, but, then, it's no use just going out once and thinking you've cracked it for another seven years.'

'Right-ho.'

'Actually, put a spoon of sugar in mine.'

'I didn't know you took sugar.'

'Nor do I. You never know until you try.'

And she looks at me and smiles. Strange days are beginning; I can feel it, strange but not unwelcome. We drink our tea, and she says,

'Of course! We'll go down to the games room! Cleaning starts tomorrow, and I want you to see it before and after.'

'Is that wise?'

'Harry. We're going down to the games room, not hiking to Mordor. Finish your tea and let's go.'

She flips out a phone, something else I have never seen her do. She presses a button, holds the little soap-bar-sized unit to her ear and says,

'Craig? We're ready now.'

She flips the machine and slaps it into her pocket as though it were a naughty elf. I exclaim,

'Craig?'

'Yes. He is going to watch out and make sure everything is

okay.'

'Why wouldn't everything be okay?'

'Stop being stubborn, you old mule.'   .

'I am not a mule! I'm a lion. I'm king of the jungle. Declan says so. Or a bear. One of the two, or maybe a strange hybrid of—'

'Come on. We're going outside.'

And I am hustled and bustled and jostled and throstled to the door and bloody well through it, and there I am, Ahab standing on the deck looking out at the mighty spume and spray, and we totter along, me like Roosevelt at Yalta and Estrella like his nurse. I don't know how we get downstairs, but we get downstairs, and then…roses.

I don't know what happened next. Estrella had her arm round my waist as the world swam away, and I leaned on my stick to keep myself from falling. Tears stream down the dry old riverbeds of my cheeks. There are roses. The last time I was standing outside my front door seven years ago, I was still mad as a march hare, as a hatter, as the mist and snow. Now it seems as though sanity is here in the shape of roses. I hear Estrella saying in my ear, her head on my shoulder,

'Oh, Harry. Harry.'

The world settles, like snow on a pine tree, and I am walking, walking. Estrella is hovering, Craig has arrived in all his unbelievable bulk, saying,

'Everyfinkay, Mr. Vanikin. Strella sessu wongo games room innit. Wuse goods lift.'

I know that this is a special dispensation, Craig being the only person able to use the goods lift, and the passenger lift being part urinal, part ghost-train. I walk slowly, using the stick, anyway, feeling afraid of falling. The light baffles me, shadows lurking among themselves like deadbeats waiting for a gang-boss to throw them a ticket for a day's work at the dockside.

Estrella seems to know where I want to go. We arrive at the goods lift, and Craig lets us in with great ceremony, sliding the clattering concertina doors closed with a titanic crash. The sound takes getting used to, as any sound above the ticking of my clock does. The loudest phenomenon the world has offered me for seven years — not counting my three days post-appendectomy — is Declan O'Riordan.

The beast descends with a lurch, arriving a few seconds later with a shuddering and indecisive shiver. Craig opens the door, and we go out into the sunlight. Estrella, dearest girl, produces a pair of sunglasses, gentleman's and cheap of provenance but essential, and puts them on me as we approach the roses.

We stop and look at the roses, the bushes placed by Craig in a good approximation of something done with care and attention, and I have a sudden spasm of Cartesian fear that this is really a dream. It has the over-real quality that convinces many a child — and some adults — to void their bladders in the sea, run priapic through the streets, speak in tongues at the foot of the stair in their underwear and teeth out.

The roses are different colours, peach and pastel, imperial purple, little Caesars, deep reds like arterial blood caught in mid-splash.

I stand, and I have stopped crying. I ask Estrella if we can have a rose to take back. Should we? Is it a crime to cut a rose on the full? No, she says, it will only die out here, unloved, unseen, born to waste its sweetness on the estate air, or words to that effect. Craig, at Estrella's prompt, produces a surely illegal knife and cuts a rose, a creamy sand colour, and gives it to me. I give to Estrella and start crying again. Then, as drunks, accident victims, and murderers say, I can't remember anything else.

CHAPTER EIGHTEEN

Dinner with Estrella

Light. A kaleidoscope of formless motion. Sound. Whisperings and murmurings but no meaning. A feeling of lightness and infinite mass. Newborn, *verfallen*, came down the dustpipe, always just arriving, late for the train, early to bed, early to rise. The clock ticks still, and a thousand seconds march towards and away from old beached Vanikin.

But then, a voice settles, meaning returns like a favourite aunt at Christmas. The voice is unfamiliar. Is it one of my own? No.

'So, he hadn't been out for…seven years. Is that right?'

'Except for the hospital.'

'What happened then?'

'His appendix burst.'

'Yes, well, he won't remember much about all that. Anaesthesia, minister to pain as she is, and what have you. That will seem like a dream.'

'Will he be okay?'

'The thing is, Miss…'

'Harte.'

'The thing is, Miss Harte, long-term agoraphobics can't just pop out to the shops every seven years for some milk and cigs. They have to be prepared for it mentally.'

'By psychologists?'

'No, Miss Harte. Not by psychologists. Psychologists are

wankers on stilts. Excuse my language, but you only have to watch your mouth if you are NHS. We can say what we like, and if you don't like it, you can't say you're paying my wages with your tax money.'

'So, what do we do, doctor?'

'How long have those blinds been up?'

'The whole seven years.'

'Right. Well, when he's up and about, they are coming down.'

'I could do that now!'

'No! He has to do it. Right. What does he eat? Crap, I expect.'

'Someone does his shopping for him.'

'What, makes his decisions as to what he eats for him?'

'No.'

'So, he eats crap.'

'Tinned food, mostly.'

'So, crap. Can you cook?'

'Yes.'

'And you are a good friend, right?'

'I…I think so. I try to be'.

'Well, you can be a good friend now. Make him stews, broths, ragouts. Bit of salad, but don't go mad, it's over-rated. Avocadoes, bananas, I'll make a list. Don't worry. I might drink a lot, but I know what he should eat. Does he drink?'

'No.'

'Christ. Puts him in a minority of one here, I should imagine. Well, he wants a glass of wine a day. And no supermarket crap. Has he got money? I imagine he has because his sister hired me, and I know she has.'

'Yes.'

'Right. There is a good vintner near here. I'll give you the address and make a list. Tell them I sent you. You might get a trade discount on the Malbec and the *Gigondas*. Miss Harte?'

'Yes, doctor?'

'Don't be put off by me. Nice doctors don't cure people. It's little shits like me that do that.'

'I have to ask you something important.'

'Now's your chance. Seize it.'

'Harry — Mr. Vanikin — used to be a teacher.'

'I know.'

'Well, he's due to be one again. We were going to start a school here.'

'When?'

'A week today. That was going to be the first lecture. Now, I suppose that's all ruined.'

'Balls. It's an excellent idea. Perfect. Gives him something to aim at. A horizon. It will focus him when he comes round. He only fainted. Hyperoxygenisation, I suspect.'

'Oh, wonderful!'

'Can I come?'

'Come to what?'

'To the lecture.'

'Well, we can't pay you. Well, we could…'

'In my free time, Miss Harte.'

'Estrella.'

'Estrella. When I'm not working, I'm usually in the pub, and I could do with a change.'

'Yes. I'll let you know the exact date.'

'Good. Right! One more thing.'

'Yes?'

'You care for him, don't you?'

'Yes.'

'Do you know why?'

'Yes.'

'Why?'

There is a long pause. Then,

'My father was a fucking bastard. I want a new one.'

'Good. Excellent. I'll write those lists.'

The voices recede, sleep returns, the sandman, with a chopper to chop off your head. In the clouds. Cloud 9. *Nein, nein! Verstanken!* Here we go round the mulberry bush. Sleep.

When I awake again, things are a good deal clearer. I think I must have been given a sedative. Estrella is fussing around in the kitchen area. Any property that contains 'areas' is essentially always going to be one room and a toilet. They draw the line at a toilet area. Estrella approaches the bed like a bird-watcher creeping up to a nest of rare chickadees.

'Harry?'

'Hello, Estrella. What happened?'

'You fainted. By the roses.'

'I thought I must have done.'

'The doctor says we took you out a bit too quickly.'

'I think I heard you talking. Who is that doctor?'

'He's private. Your sister arranged it.'

Well, Vanikin goes private. Is that against my principles? Do I have principles? Those of Seneca and Marcus Aurelius, I would hope, but quite probably those of a corrupt market trader, like everyone else in these treacherous times. I say,

'Has this spoiled everything?'

'No! And even if it had, it wouldn't have been your fault.'

'Well, I did stay in my room for seven years, so it sort of is.'

Why am I speaking as though I were fifteen? Perhaps it is beginning, the great regression, as Vanikin reaches the apogee of his manhood and begins to cycle backwards, like those great trick-cyclists, towards infancy via adolescence, only travelling at breakneck speed, downhill not to the grave but the cradle. Estrella says,

'It will soon be supper time. Guess what we're having?'

'I've only got one plate. And one bowl.'

'That must be why I had to bring my own. And my own wine-glasses.'

'Wine?'

'The doctor says you are to have a glass of red wine a day. I have bought a lovely one from somewhere called Bazas. I mean, I didn't go to Bazas to buy it, but it didn't come from Ahmed's.'

'Oh. Right. Do I have to eat in bed?'

'No. But you have to get up slowly.'

'Ah. Right.'

So it is that Vanikin the invalid eases himself out of his sick-bed in instalments, with his nurse standing anxiously by to watch for dizziness, shaking, or any other indications that the frame is less than upright and motile. I make it into the dining area and take my seat. The table is set for two. Matching deep plates and cutlery. Two wine glasses stand to attention. None of these are my belongings, but I feel no sense of intrusion. Then, I notice the smell. How could I not have previously? Estrella has used a huge cauldron of a pot — again, not mine — to make something indescribably wonderful, a stew of some description, swimming in dark meats and healthily bouncing vegetables, all in a sumptuous gravy. She produces a ladle and takes my plate, which she fills modestly. I think of my mother and her own ladle, of Russian provenance and shiny with use and washing.

Yes, I have considered the possibility of Estrella as a mother substitute, and no, she bloody well isn't. To paraphrase Freud, with his grimly bearded face and his recreational cocaine, sometimes a ladle is just a ladle. She serves me up a patient's portion, and I dig in. It is one of the best meals I have ever tasted. I say,

'This is marvellous.'

'Thank you. I learnt to cook.'

'At mother's knee?'

'No. My mother was a terrible cook. She never saw a vegetable that didn't have to be boiled to within an inch of its life.'

'Don't tell me they taught you it in school. I thought they had done away with that sort of thing.'

'They have. Women cooking is just a front for the evil patriarchy. No. I learnt from the internet.'

'I thought that was for pornography and shopping.'

'You're very cynical, Harry.'

'Sorry.'

'No, I like it. What else can you be? It's a horrible world.'

'Well, it was too much for me.'

'You'll be fine. The doctor told me what to do.'

'Where did he come from?'

'Well, his mummy's tummy, I suppose. Like the rest of us. No, your sister arranged it all.'

A stab of guilt gets through Vanikin's defences, circumvents his shield, and stabs to his brittle and desiccated old heart.

'Ah. I see.'

'She loves you, Harry. In her own strange way.'

'She is strange, isn't she?'

'We all are.'

We eat. Estrella manhandles — womanhandles? — the wine bottle and, with the aid of a corkscrew that certainly doesn't belong to me, extricates the cork with a toothsome plop. She pours.

'There. When was the last time you had wine?'

'Um, probably the late eighteenth century.'

'I can quite believe that.'

Vanikin taking an exploratory sip, like Dr. Jekyll trying out the serum for the first time.

'Oh. It's wonderful.'

'That doctor has incredible taste. He went and got this wine while you were sleeping.'

I eat more. And more. Somehow, I don't think this meal came in a tin. I say,

'No more tinned food, eh?'

'No more tinned food. From now on, we get you on a proper diet. A teacher has to have proper food.'

'What did he say about that?'

'He wants to come.'

'What?'

'Yup. He's coming to the first lesson. How's it going?'

'Very well. Did you find anything else?'

'Loads. And some great pictures. I found a painting of the marshes where Europa House is now.'

'Is this an improvement?'

'No. I don't think anything built after about 1947 was an improvement.'

'Why does the world have to be ugly?'

'Ha! You sound like a little boy. "Mummy, why does there have to be war?"'

'Oh, no. I know the answer to that one.'

'Which is?'

'Because the world has to be ugly.'

We eat on, both slipping neatly into the rhythm and cadence of eating and talking in agreeable company. The wine seems to be the melody line to the meal's ground-note. I say,

'Heart.'

'Excuse me?'

'Your name is Heart.'

'Yes. H-A-R-T-E. Like the deer in old poems.'

'Estrella Harte. Have you got a middle name.'

And she blushes. It's quite a sight, the pale cheeks suffused with a dusky rouge like a painter's preparatory *gouache* for a sunrise. She says,

'Did you hear all of our conversation?'

'Only some. I thought it was a dream. Why, were there bits I shouldn't have heard?'

'No. He's nice. He swears a lot, but he's nice.'

'Anyway, don't change the subject.'

She smiles and eats and drinks, eats and drinks and smiles.

'Rosamund.'

'My goodness. You sound like your family owns a county somewhere.'

'Have you?'

'Have I what?'

'Got a middle name.'

'Yes. Pavel.'

'Wow. Your family was Russian, yes?'

'From Odessa. The Russian bit.'

'I think we all come from immigrants.'

'I blame boats. If the Egyptians had never invented them, we'd all be stuck at home.'

'Aeroplanes now.'

'I do know about aeroplanes, Estrella. And telephones and the motor-car and long-playing records and everything. I'm not a time-traveller from Regency times.'

She smiles again.

'Oh, yes, you are.'

We eat on in amused silence. I say,

'Please, miss. May I have some…more?'

'Yes, you may. As you have cleaned your plate. Don't get too full, though. There is dessert.'

Vanikin gets a second helping, a good boy in a bad world.

I say,

'Did you like the doctor?'

'He is funny and a good doctor who knows he is a flawed human being.'

'Socrates *and* Hippocrates *and* Aristophanes. *Goodness.*'

'I would love to know if he is married. He wasn't wearing a ring.'

Again, we eat on in silence. She says, as though reaching into the tattered book of my scurrilous mind with a candle the better to read,

'I know what you are thinking, and, no, I don't find him attractive.'

'Was I thinking that?'

'Yes.'

'Well, people are either married or they aren't.'

'Wrong. You can be both at the same time.'

It seems the preamble to something else, so I hold my tongue, nothing like as easy as it sounds. She continues,

'I was married. Well, not actually, but same as makes no difference. Have you ever been married, Harry?'

I chew ruminatively on a piece of meat and look up into the corner of the room as though it held a key to mysteries. I say,

'Yes. Yes, I have.'

CHAPTER NINETEEN

Of First and Last Editions

I met my wife at a symposium on the Renaissance. The philosopher and the historian. Quite appropriate, really. We had both sat through a rather pompous lecture by that ass Julian Welberry on da Vinci, Michelangelo, Lorenzo Medici, and the politics of artistic patronage, and were snaffling up a spot of lunch before shuffling off to our next appointment, Maria de Cesare on alchemy and Aristoteleanism — rather good, actually — when a mutual friend introduced us over quiche and perfunctory salad. Personally, I could have done with some proper peasant chow, the other side of the Renaissance, where the real people lived. I think I still carried some vestigial remains of my youthful minor Socialism then. The fire is fully extinguished now.

We were having a little symposium all our own, the four of us, eating terrible and very un-Italian food in the converted Trestevere farmhouse in which we sat. One of our party — not the mutual friend, who was a linguist — was an economist, and was making an improving point to the effect that, with patronage as an expression of pre-modern capitalism, without it, there would be bugger all of note to fill the art galleries of Europe. Money not only talks, it paints, too.

Clara was pretty rather than beautiful, a Raphael flower-maid rather than a Cimabue damsel or a fat-arsed Reubens roustabout. She talked about urban conurbations and the concentration of wealth as the Italian city-states jostled for position prior to the inevitable unification. The linguist talked about art as symbolism and the grammar which dictated its use, and I chipped in my two bobs' worth concerning Giovanni Pico della Mirandola's notion of the freedom of God's greatest creation — us, supposedly — in the great *Oration on the Dignity of Man*, and how that contributed to the break with religious themes in the Renaissance, and we all had a jolly good time.

We all met up in the bar later and drank fine Tuscan wine and talked some more. Thus, for the academic, are friendships forged. Friendships and more. Clara and I 'hit it off', as young people used to say before text-speak became their lexicon. We had a mutual love of Herodotus and Schopenhauer, cross-disciplinary pollination which seemed naturally to lead to other activities undertaken by birds and bees the world over. Once back in England — I taught in London while she was an Oxford don — we would meet by the Thames or the Isis and let those rivers' waters find their natural course.

We married in springtime, as young lovers will, and set up home in the northern suburbs of London, as young lovers have ceased to do, preferring the squalid churn of the city against which to set their amatory destinies. Clara had easy access to Oxford by car, and I — not being a driver — could take a bus to the very last tube station on the line and proceed in a south-easterly direction beneath the sprawling, snarling metropolis to my place of work.

Our marriage was everything you would expect from a union of two classicists, and nauseating to the non-academic, I would imagine. Her Latin was vastly superior to mine, and she would have to explain some of her quotations, while my Ancient Greek had the edge over hers. We traded more than just life stories and pillow talk, she becoming fascinated with Lucretius and Vanikin forming a lifelong love of Suetonius. We were very much in love.

Children did not impinge on our happiness, and this for biological rather than prudential reasons. Clara had some internal complication while the Vanikin spermatozoa seemed about as willing to work as contemporary British youth. Having uncertain futures in terms of the cuts to academia making themselves known even back in the flared-trousered 1970s, we decided against adoption and, instead, made a tremendous fuss of Clara's nieces, Yevgeny not being scheduled to make his dread appearance for another decade or so but undoubtedly planning tortures and betrayals somewhere in the ether. Our children were philosophy and history, quite adorable and mischievous enough to be getting on with.

Academia took us around Europe, and we became surprisingly well travelled. Paris, Milan, even Bratislava for a weekend seminar on Eastern European historical logic, a subject which never really seemed to get its hooks into that part of the world. At home, Clara worked on her book, *Theses and Thorns: The Texts of the Reformation*, and I wrote for various journals on Plato, Hegel, Locke, all the old gang of my fascinations. We were happy, so very happy, right up until the day she left in her red Mini-Minor for Oxford, and we kissed goodbye, full of plans for a weekend in the Lake District. She never got to Oxford.

One rarely hears the rather descriptive phrase 'jack-knife', and until that day I suppose I had always been aware of its existence as a noun, never as a verb. But that is what the pantechnicon truck did, apparently, hydroplaning on a bend slick with new rain, before it batted Clara's funny little car into an oak tree and killed her. She died immediately on impact, the coroner said. Funny how one can get solace from the death of a loved one. No suffering. The ones who remain get on with all that. It rained at the funeral, and, for me, it would never stop raining.

I moved out of the house. I never could live with ghosts. Moved out, and moved in to the house of philosophy, wandering its corridors like an unquiet spirit, festering in the mired dung-heap that would eventually grow an academic *fleur du mal* that would lead to a death of sorts all its own, as I was defenestrated from my university. Then, I went mad. Then, I came here. The rest, you know, gentle reader. Here's to the underworld. I'll let you know if I find Eurydice. I have never talked about Clara until this moment, and, to my great surprise, no tears come. I think Clara might have admired that. Estrella says,

'Oh, Harry. I can't say I'm sorry because I hate it when people say that.'

'So do I. Might I have a little more wine?'

'Of course.'

Estrella pours and says,

'Well, since I don't know what to say, I'll just say that it feels like it's my turn now.'

'If you feel you want to.'

'I don't. But it just feels like I should. No one died, though.'

'Small mercies.'

'I had a boyfriend. We grew up together, and we did everything together. When we were both sixteen, he took my virginity, and I took his.'

Estrella is talking easily, with the practiced cadence of someone retelling a well-worn and well-known tale, like Greeks sitting around a beacon fire reciting Homer for the next generation. But something else tells me she has never told anyone what she is about to tell me, no one except herself, told again and again and again like a player-piano on repeat.

'We never got married because it was always so obvious we would one day, anyway, so we just never got around to it.

Which made things easier in the end.'

Knowing, having been forewarned, that death was not the end, I knew it had to be life's omnipresent other, love or, at the very least, sex, love's evil twin. Estrella stops and says,

'Dessert! I'm not telling my life story without some pudding! Now, before you get too impressed, I didn't make this. I bought it. It's really unhealthy, and you can only have a bit because you're poorly, and the doctor would spit feathers if he knew I was giving it to you.'

She clears away the detritus of our main course, re-fills our glasses — I hope she's not trying to get me drunk — and opens the fridge door to retrieve what, in the context of my fridge, must be more or less its entire contents. She places it in the centre of the table — the clock has been demoted to the draining-board — and stands looking at it. It is the largest, stickiest-looking, most potential harbinger of clotted arteries and angina I have ever seen. A chocolate cake as big as the Ritz. She says,

'There!'

And it certainly is there, its *quidditas*, or 'this-ness' — Clara had once explained how Latin doesn't really allow of a better translation — is imperial, substantive in the extreme, and almost hyper-real. Ceremonially, Estrella cuts herself an extravagant slice, with a sliver for the old malingerer. She lifts her glass.

'Cheers!'

'Cheers. Can you drink wine with cake?'

'Try it.'

I do just that. The cake seems to expand my waistline with the first mouthful, sweeter and more decadent in taste than anything I remember eating before or since. Then, a small slurp of wine. Actually, this is very heaven. Strange, as I've said, times.

'Anyway, I'm not changing the subject.'

'I didn't say you were.'

'No, but I was trying to, and I am not going to let myself.'

'This cake is not like anything I have ever eaten. It feels like it is doing me no good at all, and yet, it is so good. Continue, please.'

'Well, Alex and I were obviously made for each other. That was the verdict of friends and family, and we weren't going to argue. I didn't feel the need to try a break to see what falling in love with someone else would be like, and neither did he. We didn't work at us at all. Didn't need to. So, when we had done our gap year travelling across Central America, we went to different universities. I studied English at Sussex, he went to Norwich to read physics. We'd been in each other's pockets so long, going to the same university seemed silly.'

'Sisters.'

'I beg your pardon?'

'Norwich and Sussex. They are sister universities. The same architect designed both.'

And I had lectured at both, but I deem that inconsequential in terms of Estrella's tale, which was, I fear, approaching an all-too-familiar *dénouement* in freshman circles.

'Well, that architect ought to be bloody well shot.'

'Agreed.'

'Anyway, we saw each other on breaks. I went there, or he came to me, or we both went home.'

She pauses to consume more of the ticking calorie-bomb on her plate.

'Well, I went up to UEA a day early one weekend to surprise him with a first edition of a book he loved, and it was me that got the surprise. I got there mid-evening, and as I approached his room in the halls of residence, I could hear them at it from down the corridor. She made a lot more noise fucking than I did. Maybe he liked that. I wrote a quick note on the inside cover of the book and left it outside his door. Then, I went back into Norwich town centre, went to a pub, talked to the first halfway decent-looking bloke I could find who wasn't actually prehistoric, went back to his place, and slept with him. I got up in the morning, wrote another note, and got the early train back to London.'

Silence. Silence and cake. I say,

'A weekend of notes.'

'Yes. False notes.'

'Did you ever hear from him again?'

'He sent so many emails I had to close down the account and start another one. If I go home now, I always check with my mother to make sure he isn't around.'

Cake. Wine. I say,

'Well, I can't say I'm sorry, either.'

'No.'

'But you've seen other people since?'

'Yes. And it lasts about as long as I can stand not being able to stand seeing them go out the door. I have what they call trust issues.'

'That was one of the best meals I have ever had, Estrella.'

'Thank you.'

'No, no more wine for me. I had better introduce myself to that as cautiously as I do to standing up.'

'Well, I'm going to take the bottle home and finish it.'

She kisses me on the cheek and is gone. Death and the maiden.

CHAPTER TWENTY

Let the Games Begin

'Let there be light,' saith the Lord, and Lo, there was light. 'More light,' said Goethe on his death-bed, and then expired, hopefully getting his wish. 'I shall believe', said the doubting Descartes, 'only that which is shown to me by the natural light of the mind.' My task, where light is concerned, is somewhat simpler. Estrella takes one end of the huge black theatre curtain, which has seen its last performance of this particular run — Vanikin! The Musical! — and we pull on a count of three. I wonder if God counted to three before he created the universe. If so, in which language? I suppose it is, as the Bible says, one of the things which is hid. A bit like Vanikin's little sandpit, until…

Three!

The gentlemen fancifully mentioned in an earlier episode as the designers of the behemoth which is Europa House, and their discussions on the orientation of the building with regard to the sun, unknowingly did old Vanikin proud. Helios, in all his glory, is pouring forth in my general direction. If Stonehenge really was a giant act of worship to the pagan sun-god, and had it been built on the marshes of Bermondsey instead of in rural Wiltshire, the key-stone would have been planted just where I am standing. The sun. Now there is a god really worth worshipping. No *deus absconditus* there. A deity which always turns up on time and does what is asked of it.

Estrella is doing a fair bit of beaming herself.

'Oh, Harry! Isn't it beautiful? I hardly get the sun.'

The ancients did, I muse, but let the moment pass. I say,

'Shows up a multitude of sins, though.'

What's with, as the young people say, all the religious imagery today? Don't tell me Vanikin is getting God. No. I haven't found God. Let him find me. If, as claimed, he is omnipresent, then he knows where I live. I say,

'Perhaps I should decorate.'

'Um, no. I wouldn't bother. Just needs a bit of a clean. Magda will probably be overjoyed. Ooh! That reminds me. Back in a tick.'

And Estrella, full now with plans and projects, is a whirling dervish (dervishess?) of motion these days. She disappears and leaves me alone with my clock, restored to its fealty in the middle of the table. How many ticks and tocks has it seen? And how much has happened during the last few thousand? Time, writes old Kant, is the condition of our experience, and I suppose it does have a fairly big say in things, for all its vagaries and uncertainties. And so, the minute-hand, clunking into place every sixty seconds, as though the minute itself came and went all at once, ruled all. George Eliot, with her man's pen-name and problems with Nietzsche, writes that 'development and catastrophe can often be measured by nothing clumsier than the moment-hand.'

And now Estrella is back, bearing what looks to be a large square of plastic, mainly because that is what it is, but a square of plastic doubling as the portal to the modern world. Vanikin enters the computer age. Estrella says,

'Now. Where shall we put the clock? We need to find something to put it on. I'll get you something from the charity shop. A little chest or something.'

'Putting time on a pedestal. Is that wise?'

'Better than putting people on one.'

'Now that is true.'

She moves the clock to its current holiday home, its temporary *dacha*, on the draining-board. On the table, she places what I believe is termed a 'laptop.' Ought it not to be on her lap, like an Edwardian dowager's Pekingese?

'Here, I want to show you something.'

We sit in front of her machine, and she commands it regally with its keyboard. A photograph, slightly blurred but with detail enough, fills the screen. She presses a small arrow in the corner, and it becomes clear that this is a moving picture.

If it is a feature film, it seems to be a low-budget art-house movie, art-house being that type of cinema generally presented in the more obscure European languages, sub-titled in *slightly* imperfect English and aimed at an audience comfortable with scenes that last over three seconds. We open on what look like, what are, double doors held locked by a sturdy chain and impressive padlock. There is a kerfuffle while the cameraman, or camerawoman, or cameraperson fumbles to open the padlock, and the doors swing open onto darkness. A light is flicked on, and a scene of squalid poverty, neglect, and disorder greets the viewer.

The camera moves slightly jerkily into the interior, and the full jumble of manically discarded household goods, severely injured ping-pong tables, cardboard boxes, bloated black bin-liners, upside-down and deranged dollies, odd and unwearable shoes, and all the detritus of the underclass appears like a moonscape or amateur news footage of a terrorist attack on a church-hall jumble sale.

As the camera roves over the piles of rubbish, tin cans, upended ashtrays, beer cans and broken bottles, gruesomely dismembered children's toys, and other consumable goods that have passed the event horizon after which they become what our transatlantic cousins call 'trash,' I begin to wonder what the *dénouement* of this brutalist slice of *cinema verité* will be. Estrella pauses the film, the frozen scene showing an extravagantly and imaginatively graffitied wall featuring a woman's name accompanied by a claim concerning her amatory exploits. Estrella says,

'Do you know where that is?'

'Beirut? The Democratic Union of the Congo?'

'No and no. It's the games room downstairs.'

'Oh, Estrella. Where are we going to go?'

'For what?'

'The lessons. The school.'

'See the date?'

She pointed at a series of numbers at the top of the screen. I decoded them.

'That's two days ago. How can we use that?'

'Get your shoes on, and grab your walking-cane.'

'But wha—'

'And put your sunglasses on. It's bright out there.'

'I don't have any sunglasses.'

At this, she reaches into the pocket of her jacket and produces the same pair of rather stylish, albeit cheap, gentleman's sunglasses, which she put on me before, and this time, before I have a chance to protest, they are in place. She claps her hands.

'Chop-chop!'

I do as I am bid. I put on my best jacket, a sort of cross between a wine waiter's livery and a yachting conceit, with a white shirt underneath. Once I have the stick and the glasses on, I look like Claude Rains in *The Invisible Man* going in search of his bandages. With Estrella as my escort, taking my arm like a rich man's floozy, we stroll on deck.

As we pace the silent walkways, everyone either asleep,

watching television, or out doing God knows what — and this whatever the time of day or night — I feel that I am privy to exactly what you're thinking. Estrella's laptop is in my apartment. If someone saw her take it there, then surely — as I have apprised you of the desultory nature of my castle's defences, as it were — someone would instantly break the door down and steal it, theft between council flats being simply a (non-) occupational hazard of living here in the underworld. However, by a strange quirk, a glitch in the common reality of the criminal world, a rent in the fabric of what is and shall be, we don't suffer from the usual nightmarish spate of inter-flat burglary here at Europa House, and this is due to Craig's saving grace. Hasn't everyone got one? How would they be saved else?

The last time anyone here 'tried it on,' to use the argot, Craig simply called his brothers, Russell and Lee. They apprehended the criminal, a man called Teriyaah Catkins, and took him to the boiler room under house arrest. There, they suspended him upside-down for a day, allowing him no food, water, or sleep. They would wet his lips with vinegar, like Christ, whenever it seemed he may actually expire from the heat. Then, they let him go, with instructions to tell his co-workers how he spent his weekend. There has been no repeat of this transgression since. We are, curiously, safer than some of the upper middle class, the bank CEOs, and pop stars of London, in their gated communities. Life is rich and strange, and you can't tell me it isn't.

'Such are my thoughts,' wrote Plato in the — disputed — Seventh Letter, 'as I enter Syracuse.' Only, we aren't going to Syracuse; we are going to the games room. We stop briefly by the roses so that I might see and smell them — and to make sure I am not going to keel over again, I'm sure — and make our way across the courtyard to the games room, which I had never visited in person but had, as you know, viewed the promotional video. We stop at the familiar double doors. Estrella says,

'Ready?'

I am, and say as much. I want to add that I think Estrella is over-estimating my — our — new-found powers. I may be dressed as though I am playing Howard Hughes in an amateur theatrical production, but I can't wave a financial wand and transfer the urban pandemonium I have recently viewed on the magic lantern of the cinema everyone now owns. Craig appears, stage left, like the bastard love-child of a pantomime genii and a sumo wrestler. He says, I believe he says,

'Good morning, Mr. Vanikin. Nice to see you up and about, sir.'

'How can I know,' writes that old doubter Descartes — before he discovered the light-switch mentioned in dispatches earlier — 'that I am not dreaming, and that which I see is not real?' Craig produces a bunch of keys that have presumably gone missing from the Tower of London, and proceeds to open the padlock holding closed the doors to the games room.

The colour strikes me first. The walls, the ceiling. Estrella says that she asked Suze Kennett for advice, Suze being a tattoo-artist. I struggle to see the relevance, but Estrella says Suze knows her colour-wheel. The walls and ceiling are a pollen sunflower yellow, as though the sun has given them a light dusting in passing.

The rubbish, the sheer mounds of stained and ugly detritus, like essence of poverty, I had seen on the short camera footage was gone. The place even smells pleasant. There are chairs, ranged neatly and pointing to a central locus, where the teacher would stand, will stand, the vanishing point, the Vanikin point. Estrella had said not a word since we had come in, and Craig is acting like the humble janitor at the Sistine Chapel when Michelangelo wanted to pop round for a quick check-up on his ceiling. I say to Estrella,

'Who cleared up? The council?'

'Local authority, Harry. And no, they didn't. Everyone here cleared up. Europa House cleared up.'

I have nothing to say. This is a time when words are uninvited guests at a party which was going just swimmingly without them. I feel a bit misty-eyed and am glad when Mrs. Pallis arrives with Jimmy-Shawn as a sort of bearer, with bottles of water with which he loads a fridge in the corner. Mrs. Pallis speaks, as much like a colonial-era bingo-caller as ever,

'Don't anyone be late for school tomorrow!'

For tomorrow is, indeed, the first day of school.

CHAPTER TWENTY-ONE

Entry of the Gladiators

So, then. A teacher's day. I try to search through the old sock-drawer of memory for the last time I actually taught anyone anything. Over seven years ago, obviously. Would I still have the knack? Estrella thought so, as did the rest of my would-be class here at Europa House. Don't let them down, Vanikin! Europa House expects...

Estrella makes us lunch before school, the lesson being due to begin at 2:00 p.m. in order to consolidate and accommodate the various lifestyles of today's pedagogical subject matter, Europa House. Mrs. Pallis, for example, would most likely be up at about 5:00 a.m. for a few lines from the Good Book and to make breakfast for Jimmy-Shawn and Qaneesha. Co-simultanously, Declan and Marek would be arriving home seeking their beds, doubtless after a night of Bacchanalian excess featuring a few lines of their own. All human life, as noted *passim*, is here.

In dietary terms, Estrella seems to have gone from a heathland rabbit to a savannah cougar in about a week. The predominant mood-music in her culinary efforts today is less of the bitter herbs of the common land and more Antipodean rump. We are eating bloody meat washed down with bloody wine, and she makes no secret as to why.

'You, Harry Vanikin, have done nothing more strenuous than pull on socks, read books you keep in the bath, and spoil omelettes for seven years. Today, you have to teach for an hour, and you need some sustenance.'

She looks at me as though I were a damp puppy.

'Is that okay? Just to make it an hour? First one, and everything.'

I feel something, and I know what it is, and I know why it affects me so. Someone is trying to protect me, and that was one of the many, multi-faceted, and sparkling roles Clara played in my life, unasked, unbidden. Clara was no soaring eagle, no magnificent frigate-bird, but a protective and sharp-elbowed rook, protecting the dowdy and doddering old London pigeon Vanikin from the taunts and pecks of the other birds. Except, of course, that, by the time *The Decadent Turn* had hung, overdrawn, and quartered my salary, Clara had been inconsiderate enough to have died horribly in a high-speed motorway smash. Hey ho. Life. Its details.

'Yes. That's okay.'

'*Harry*! I'm not being Mummy. What is the meat like?'

'Sumptuous. Probably too rich for my poor old tumkin.'

She looks as though someone has just goosed her.

'*What* did you say?'

I look at her as I would a linguist, or a wine-waiter at a Vienna Circle piss-up, as one might say, which part of what I said? She echoes,

'*Tumkin?*'

Well, frankly, yes. Tumkin. My tummy-tumkin. I think it may be time just to go mad again. I say,

'My mother used to say it. If I had been ill. How's your little tumkin?'

She smiles, amused and solicitous of anything that maintains my mood of general cheerfulness and trepidation, mixed but not mixed, like the balsamic vinegar and olive oil they put on tables in restaurants. Estrella says,

'Your mother used to say it.'

'Yes. Little tumkin.'

Now I do get a broad smile out of the girl, and something occurs to me. This is not 'about,' as politicians were saying last time I was on the out, simply Vanikin, with or without his tumkin. This isn't just the comeback kid, one last blag for the old criminal, like in the movies. Estrella, too, is becoming someone new, the next stage of her personal voyage from pupa to chrysalis to butterfly. Cheers!

And so, lunch wears on, and we talk about the structure things will take. I enjoy this bit because, underneath it all, she does think I am some blundering, tottery old Magoo in a once-burgundy dressing-gown. But no, there was always another Vanikin, ready to step from the shadows like one of those super-hero Johnnies who only has to whop a walking-stick on the ground, or fiddle with a trinket to turn into Vanikin Man.

I know what I am going to do, and so does she. Decent teachers can understand how the other works, like sportsmen and jazz musicians.

Well, that is lunch, as cricket umpires used to — I hope still do — say. Cricket always looked a likely lad for the cull when sports went the way of pop music, and it was required that it be produced for adult-children. The last game I remember being vaguely aware of on some bawling TV was obviously taking place at night, as the combatants were playing in their pyjamas.

The weather seems clement as we make our way to Craig's service lift, as noted, the equivalent of what was once known in some circles as 'a limo to the gig.' And, suddenly, we are at and inside the games room. A full games room, hushed in reverence. And I am here, Harry Vanikin, for a lecture. It takes me back down the penny arcade of memory.

I think I lived for lectures during my truncated academic career. Undoubtedly, ego had a part to play — it is an insistent imp — but it wasn't the ego of a lecturer, to give just one example, who turned up to a lecture with his leather jacket slung over his back and swigging on a can of lager. The lengths some lecturers went to for adulation — and after-hours solicitation with easily led students, I wouldn't wonder, says a rather Victorian Vanikin — was indicative of the combination of television and the ability to see gaudy pop-stars perform in your own living-room. But I have wandered from the path of Parmenides.

The games room is full.

And now, good people, we will exercise authorial prerogative and just leave scrawny Vanikin, dangling from a light-beam apparent organised by Craig and looking like a rubber key-ring skeleton on a fishhook. As the first painting of the marshland that preceded Europa House — *circa* 1687 — appears on the rear wall, I say,

'Welcome to Europa House…'

You have already had the two-and-sixpence tour around Europa House and its geographical environs, a sneak preview of Vanikin's great peroration. I shan't put you through it again. Suffice to say that a combination of Vanikin's old skills coming back flickeringly, like an old twinkly snooker player still taking a frame off the new kid in town, and a general air of amazement and an almost carnivalesque fascination with a spectacle which, as it was not represented on a screen, was not mundane, violent or somehow connected with the judicial system.

I wasn't Olivier in *The Entertainer*, I mean; it wasn't the return of the great song-and-dance man. I just gave a potted history of Europa House — accompanied pictorially thanks to Estrella's good offices — that poured-concrete warehouse and red-brick in which we are stored, and how this place came to be, charnel-house and home sweet home as it simultaneously is.

And something happens.

I had been dreading a breakdown of law and order. Estrella had told me some of the riper stories from her friend Sarah — a much-appreciated consultant who has herself turned up, no doubt to appraise if not to praise — and teaching nowadays sounds like a hybrid of herding cats and directing traffic in Nairobi. But there is silence, concentration, even some *note-taking*, for heaven's sake. This, to my utter amazement, is working…

At the end, there are fun and frolics, junketing and jollity. The ladies Pallis, Podolski, and Schumpeter had combined forces to produce a spread of sandwiches and cheesecake and assorted dietary hazards and treats, tea flows like wine, and Declan — to my certain knowledge — has had nothing narcotic nor alcoholic introduced to his system for at least an hour and half. He says to me,

'What I loik, Mr. V., is dat I wouldn't look twice at this place if I didn't live here. I mean, it's shoite. But yew, yew made it into a story and, well, history. I s'pose that's why it's called history. 'Cos it's a story and all.'

I wonder if they will remember Vanikin as 'the man who made shite places interesting.' There could be worse obituaries. Lars claps me on the shoulder and beams and tells me well done, well done, as though I had just isolated a polymer as a member of his lab team.

Mrs. Pallis pushes Jimmy-Shawn forward like a croupier moving a roulette chip across the baize. She looks at me, and he steps forward, page penitent. He says,

'Firstly, Mr. Vanikin, thank you for the Cee Vee. Secondly, Mr. Vanikin, that was fascinating. I never knew — I didn't know all that about the house.'

Mrs. Pallis keeps her beaming counsel, ferrying off young Jimmy-Shawn to, I hope, a future free from both the police and his cultural co-conspirators.

It is all starting to blur a little, and Estrella, attentive to the doddering Vanikin like a young Raj schoolmarm — which, I suppose, is what she is — with an ageing and battle-weary pasha, hustles me out and back up to the Vanikin suite. I sleep and dream not of pleased parents or reconciliations over the decades or Clara, but of the sky. Just the sky. Non-committal blue-grey. Just sky.

When I wake, it is to the smell of cooking, as it has been for the last few days. I get up, preparatorily dressed, and take the two paces required to gain the grand ballroom. Estrella stops what she is doing, turns, moist-eyed, and gives me a hug, a sylph of the wood acknowledging the efforts of an old bear.

Later, we are eating a simple meal of pasta, salad, and one of those Italian breads which sounds like it might be a Renaissance painter. *This was the period in which Focaccia worked less for the Medicis and began to take a more secular subject matter...*

Estrella says,

'You are teaching again on Saturday. Introduction to history. I'm doing tomorrow.'

'Um, right. Okey-dokey. What are you teaching?'

'Remedial writing.'

I suspect she reads from my look that I suspect I may still be dreaming and that this is just more sky. She continues to enlighten.

'You see, Harry, none of the non-readers would have come to a class if you singled them out and made them feel they couldn't read. Now they have seen a lesson. They feel a part of it.'

'Can you teach remedial reading? I mean, you personally?'

'Bugger off, Harry. I can read. I will teach those that can't how to read, too. What, would you like me to get a licence from what you call the council?'

'No. I am happy to do it. What are we going to call it?'

She looks at me as though I have just sawn through a branch of a tree the wrong end of which I had been perched on.

'Remedial. Reading. I told you.'

'I meant the school.'

She pauses, and I seize my chance. I say,

'Harte-Vanikin!'

'Vanikin-Harte!'

'Harte-Vanikin!'

'Vanikin-Harte!'

'It was your idea!'

'Well, if it is a question of whose idea it was, we'll just call it the Mrs. Pallis school. Ooh, have you heard they're opening one of those Mrs. Pallis schools down our street?'

'Well, if it isn't your name first, I am having nothing to do with it.'

'It's too late!'

'What do you mean?'

'Get your sneakers on. I want to show you something'.

I rise Caesar-like, don my outdoor wear, and escort our young teaching assistant to the games room, ably ferried in the goods lift by Craig, who now waits as attentively as any private chauffeur for the arrival of guests. As we make our now-familiar way to Europa House's new place of learning, I see that something has been added above the door, a wooden plaque with neatly executed writing across it, stylish letters in paint which bear the legend:

EUROPA HOUSE

THE VANIKIN-HARTE SCHOOL

CHAPTER TWENTY-TWO

Term Time

And so, good reader, a place of learning is born, a tower not of ivory but 1960s pre-stressed and poured concrete and regular London brickwork, a university for the disenfranchised, disheartened, and, in some cases, dysfunctional. From our first baby steps came confident strides, and the whole added up to a giant leap.

Estrella is remarkable, from ugly duckling to swan with a few shakes of her tail feathers. The school takes up all her time, and began to take up her money, too. We had a slightly stern meeting one rainy afternoon — I can see the drops on the window-panes now — when I noticed that new whiteboards and marker pens were arriving, folders for school projects — there are school projects! — were being handed out, and 'Vanikin-Harte School' mugs started appearing during coffee breaks with a rather fetching logo apparently designed by Mrs. Schumpeter and based on a Bavarian guild crest from the seventeenth century. Estrella had been paying for things, and I made her fetch all the receipts and went through them and gave her the money back. The receipts were stapled into a book, one to a page, with a description on the page and the price and a running total. This job was allocated to our apprentice accountant, Jimmy-Shawn Pallis.

The days became weeks, the weeks months. Winter came and Christmas, and Estrella and I became quite the pedagogical partnership. I was, quite literally and under the watchful dietary eye of Estrella and Dr. Benison — for that is his name — going from strength to strength, and there were no more swoons and faints.

Then, one day early in January, Estrella appears at my door with the same regularity as my trusty clock clicks off the time, and sits with an unusual air of preoccupation, her old self *redux*. She says,

'Tomorrow's lesson. Yours, I mean.'

'Yes! Continuing with the history of the First World War, I think.'

'Yes, doesn't matter what it is. A journalist wants to come.'

'Ah. I rather thought we were keeping all this a secret so that we didn't get into trouble with the council.'

'Local authority. We were. But journalists find things out. That's what they do. Could have been one of the boys in a pub. Could have been anyone.'

'Well, do we have to let him come? Or her come?'

This makes Estrella smile as she realises that some of her ingrained political correctness had rubbed off on old Vanikin. She says,

'Him. He's been in touch. He says he is from one of the big newspapers, and I checked, and he is.'

'Oh God. They are going to dig up my past again. The book! They'll find out that's why I came here. Which I did for a quiet life.'

'Harry. It's not Watergate or The Troubles. He says he has heard good things, and I talked him through it, and I don't think it can do any harm.'

Harm. First, do no harm. The first line of the Hippocratic Oath that all doctors still — I sincerely hope — have to recite before beginning their careers. Journalists have something similar. The corollary to the good doctor. Widdershins.

Mutandis mutandis.

First, do as much harm as you can.

I want to explain to Estrella that it was journalists that ended my career, journalists that rounded on me and took me down like ants on a moth, journalists that led Vanikin here, to the underworld. What I end up saying, like a grumpy old man agreeing to have his toenails cut by nurse, is,

'Oh, alright, then!'

She says,

'Good. Right. I have a remedial arithmetic class in ten minutes. Did you know that Declan can add a string of random numbers, just thrown at him, faster than anyone I have ever seen?'

'Extraordinary. You have taught well.'

'Rubbish. He's a drug dealer, and he plays darts. Of course, he can add up. You can learn from life, Harry. It's not all just books.'

And Estrella is gone, a worker-ant nowadays instead of a sluggish caterpillar. Journalism. I have a bit of a sit down. I realise straight away, like the alcoholic's moment of clarity, why journalists frighten me, quite apart from the fact that they were the jackals that turned the media pack on to poor leveret Vanikin. No. They are a link, a portal, a passe-partout into the dread outer world. And in all fairness, that is still another country to me. Yes, I had pranced about in the courtyard and fainted by the roses and been in the Parthenon of the games room. But I still hadn't been down to the shops. I like a firm line between underworld and overworld. There is an agitation at the door, one I know well. It is Magda of the Steppes, the Witch of Prague relocated to a cleaner's cupboard in south-east London. I admit her. She sits at my invitation, makes no move to read my tarot cards, produces no crystal ball, but clearly needs to disburden herself of a hidden concern. She says,

'Mr. Vennerkin. I still cannot get used to seeing your room with the light! BUT!'

And she raises a forefinger like a sceptical countess at a roulette table, and says,

'This is not what I came to say.'

Magda looks straight at me, something she has never, to my knowledge, ever done. She says,

'If, Mr. Vennerkin, there comes a time for you to leave us, I ask that you do not forget us. Because you have brought a light, Mr. Vennerkin, like the light that through your window shines!'

Oh, Christ on a pogo-stick, she *has* been reading my fucking tarot cards. Vanikin has death in the cards! She has come to take me from the underworld to paradise. Or something. I say,

'Magda. I have no intention of going anywhere just yet.'

Perhaps it is my new-found confidence, what with being the headmaster of Europa House, but gone are the days when Magda reduced me to a monosyllabic chump. I can now string whole sentences together in her presence, spectral and redolent of Pepper's Ghost as it is. Magda says,

'We all think we see future, Mr. Vennerkin. But, really, future sees us. And thank you so much for your lecture on eastern Europe. Although, it made me little homesick. Well! Magda says enough! I must go and clean apartment of Mrs. Podolski, which is easy job because she is super-clean lady!'

And with that, Magda dematerialises, and her spirit-self glides to her next appointment, leaving poor fuddled Vanikin with much to think on.

How easily we change, and yet, how hard it is without the catalyst of others. Left alone, we are happy just to run around in our hamster-wheels. When other souls appear through the mist, suddenly the wheel doesn't seem so appealing any more.

We are not islands, or, if we are, we are part of a chain of islands, a Peloponnesian of persons, able to hop and travel, skip like flung flat-stones and recognising ourselves in the other and the other in ourselves.

But, while those others guide and direct, assist and assign, they can also give the gift of autonomy. Like the stabilisers I had on the rear wheel of my first bicycle, they helped the rider gain confidence, but, ultimately, one had to ride on one's own.

I know exactly what I have to do as the boy's signal rappity-tap sounds as what my clock designates as the appointed hour.

I am dressed in my outdoor threads, my waiter jacket and deck shoes, crisp white shirt — Mrs. Podolski insists on doing my washing now, and I am becoming something of a sink-estate Beau Brummel — and with my sunglasses showing jauntily in my top pocket, every bit as though I were a *boulevardier* at Juan-les-Pins. I admit the boy. He is still growing, as though trying to reach heaven before the rest of us. He says,

'Morning, Mr. Vanikin. Got your list?'

'No, actually.'

'Oh. Well. I think I can remember most of—'

'I'm coming with you.'

'Oh. Right. Can I just ask Estrella something?'

And he is gone, a treasonous, traitorous Mercury who thinks that Vanikin has no mind, no will of his own. Bah! Like the man in the iron mask, the prisoner of Zenda, and the birdman of Alcatraz, I yearn to be free, and so, I shall. I—

A new knock on the door, an unfamiliar one, ordered and regular. Not fate, surely. I am no Don Juan, and need no stone guest, and it is not Declan or Marek; it is no stoned guest. I open the door, unafraid now of it being Adam with his mimicry. He stopped doing that after coming to a lesson and looking at me afterwards in something of a new light. No, my visitor is our tortured writer from below Château Vanikin. It is Simon

Pilkington.

As mentioned in a previous episode, Mr. Pilkington is both a writer and every bit as reclusive as your humble scribe. I didn't exactly hear him pacing the room down there, interrupted by the tac-tac-tac of the classic typewriter, but one or two of the well informed at Europa House know more about the tenants here than Boswell knew about Johnson.

He is also, by Estrella's account, a voracious reader and, she said, often came home carrying real books. This made me rather sad, reminding me of the time I saw a bottle of lemonade on a supermarket shelf bearing the proud statement 'made with real lemons.'

And now Mr. Pilkington is here, and, as I add my own introduction, we are already on first-name terms. I offer him tea which he declines. He does not strike me as a serial abuser of alcohol, has none of the familiar semiotics one reads elsewhere in the block. Perhaps he just doesn't like tea. He seems like a man with a message demanding urgency and immediacy of delivery, like a breathless page in a Jacobean drama. I invite him to sit, and this, he does.

'Well, Professor Vanikin.'

'Harry. Please.'

'Well, Harry. I. Have been. To some of your lectures. That is the first thing I need to tell you.'

'I believe I have seen you there.'

'Yes. Yes, I was. However, I wondered if you had recorded them in any way.'

'Well, yes. Estrella set up some sort of camera device, and I believe she has the whole thing on a…some sort of…driver disc or what have you.'

'Ah, excellent! I wonder if she, or rather you, or rather both of you would mind I could watch some of the lessons by myself.'

I was at one of those odd crossroads that sometimes occur in conversations, where there are fingerposts pointing to all available paths, but none are marked. I roll the dice and say,

'Of course. Might I ask why?'

'Yes, certainly. I don't like being with a lot of people. In a crowded space.'

Other people's lives. Kaleidoscopes and wheels within wheels. I say,

'Ah, I see. I am afraid what I know about computers you could write on the back of a postage stamp with a laundry marker. But I am sure Estrella will organise it. Does she need your…email box or something?'

'It's okay. I will have a word with her. Thank you. And there was something else.'

'Absolutely!'

'Could I be considered for private tuition? I would pay you, of course. Perhaps you might need the money for the school.'

I look at S. Pilkington Esq. as though he has just sprouted celestial wings and say,

'Well, um, certainly. I mean, absolutely. That is, as long as you don't want tuition in the history of Mesopotamia or the fruit-fly. It would have to be something, um, within my field, as it were.'

'Oh, I think it is.'

'Ah, good. My area of expertise and so on.'

'I would say so.'

'Well, you seem confident enough that I can help, and, if I can, I would be glad to. Now, what exactly would you like tuition in?'

'Your book. *The Decadent Turn.* I've read it five times.'

Chapter Twenty-Three

A New Printing

My great-uncle Dmitri had a saying. 'No matter how well you plan a murder at sea,' he would say, 'if you dump the body in the water, it will always wash up somewhere.' This has absolutely no relevance to my own tale; I just like it. Actually, I retract the claim that Dmitriov's grisly, piratical tale-in-miniature has no relevance. Its relevance is its irrelevance.

What is relevant for Vanikin the Confused just at the moment? Otherness, disturbance, a straying from the norm, the ripples from a stone tossed into a mill-pond. Something is afoot.

Firstly, Estrella calmly informs me that a journalist — kryptonite to Vanikin! — is strong-arming his way into my *sanctum sanctorum*. Next, the boy disappears like a stage phantom as soon as I announce my intention of coming to Ahmed's with him! If you will! Continuing, the Witch of Endor with moth-spray, aka Magda, gazes into her ball and casually alerts me to a future possibly involving my imminent doom. And, to put the tin hat on everything, the morose and solitary writer who lives downstairs turns out to be more or less the secretary of my fan club. What times are these?

More to the point, where is my bloody shopping? I bet Plato never had to put up with this. I mean, since Estrella took over culinary duties, I don't require the military-style rations the boy would fetch at one time. Estrella does the shopping now, and I pay her. But the boy is an essential link between me and what went before. Before what? Before the Vanikin-Harte School, I suppose. BVHS, era of.

No, I'm not one of those formidably coated Russian literary malcontents or misfits, seeing the golden path shining ahead but taking the dark and suspicious back roads of the past, where danger and despair and degradation inevitably lurk. I may have Russian blood in my veins, but I have seen too much Western optimism — misplaced, as it often is — to lie down in the snow and die outside Moscow.

It's just the way things have changed. I have had too much experience with change not to notice the warning wind rustling in the sedge-grass, not to see the broken twigs in the forest, not to sniff the enemy on the wind. I think briefly of putting the theatre-curtain back up, as a gesture of defiance, a barricade, a way of saying: thus far and no further! I have a bit of a sit-down, instead. I doze, and I am woken from a dream of dark interior woodland — you don't need your *Freud for Dummies* for that one — to the new, improved, imperial, rap-di-rap-rap, RAP-RAP! of my teaching assistant.

After Estrella sits and I act with my eyebrows a bit, like a mime artist, she says,

'Oh, for God's sake. What on earth is wrong with you?'

'It's all very irregular.'

'Harry. You sound like a Health and Safety officer. Or that bloke in the tin hat from *Dad's Army.*'

'The boy refused to do my shopping!'

'No, he didn't.'

'Well, he said he had to ask you. I don't need a pass, do I? To go to the shops? Or an exit visa or something?'

'Why won't you just take advice? We can go out. Just not today.'

'Why not today?'

Estrella stands up. This is becoming like some student production of Ibsen. She says, with a motherly firmness in which I detect a frisson of humour,

'Harry Vanikin! Your life has changed immeasurably in the last few months, and I bloody well had lots to do with that. The last time you were left to your devices, you locked yourself in here for seven years. You need other people to…'

'To what?'

'Get you ready. For the world.'

'Ah. Am I someone's ward?'

'Yes, you big goon. You're mine.'

Estrella looks as though she is about to cry. I would wish that earth would swallow me up, but, of course, it already did that seven years ago, as noted. That's why I am here. It's now that I realise that without Estrella, without teaching, without the school and the people and the encouragement and the enthusiasm I would never again have left this room. I would have died here, a burden and a waste and a pointless thing, mere exercise for pall-bearers. Estrella leaves swiftly, like an onstage messenger not waiting to hear Caesar's reply. She says she will return, as she has something for me.

I sit for a while, feeling more than slightly wretched, and am genuinely pleased when I hear a knock on the door, one I recall but cannot place, meaning this is not a regular visitor. I put my jacket on. Estrella made me throw my dressing-gown away, a move I initially resisted but soon saw the wisdom in. I did suggest giving it a proper send-off, a Viking burial or similar, but she just put it in a bin-liner, and down the rubbish chute, it went. I open the door. It is the formidable figure of Marvin M. He says,

'Mr. Vanikin?'

'Um, it is I!'

'I know. I wondered if I could come in?'

This is actually rather a literalist question, as Marvin M. is, as noted in a previous episode, a man-mountain. He negotiates the logistics of his entrance, however, with a dancer's grace. With an eye to structural reliability, I motion Mr. M. — what else am I to call him? — to sit in, or rather on, my throne. I take the guest chair, and something about the situation seems not to call for a cup of tea. I break the ice.

'What can I do for you?'

He looks quizzically at me. He says,

'You mean, that you haven't done already?'

'Ah. You have enjoyed the classes.'

Marvin M. had, indeed, been at some of the classes, but Estrella and I talked about this and decided we would never pat people on the head for turning up. I understood why and agreed, even if I could not for the very life of me have told you why. The huge gentleman opposite me says,

'Mr. Vanikin. I will come straight to the point. I watch what you have done here. Then, I look at myself. You give knowledge away, Mr. Vanikin.'

'Harry. Please.'

'Harry. And please call me Marvin. You give it away. And I sell drugs, and I pimp women.'

I assume this is not a retail pitch. I say,

'I'm not judging you.'

There is a silence. It is a very personal thing to have said to such a large man associated with such an industry as his. He says,

'No. But I am judging you. And I find myself wanting.'

'Wanting?'

'Wanting. Wanting to give you a lot of money to set up more schools.'

I suppose the old Vanikin route-bus has taken a different wander around the coast of my life in recent months. But I have to say an investment offer from one of the biggest criminals in the postcode was not something I was expecting. I allow myself time to register what I have heard, but, before I can essay a reply, Marvin has a *post scriptum*.

'I know what you are thinking Mr. Vanikin. Harry. The money is dirty, and how could you take it? Well, that is a moral problem, and I understand you are a philosopher, so I suppose this is something you are able to think about.'

I look at Marvin M. This miracle of genetics, this semi-mythical, comic-book, impeccably dressed, untouchable lord of the manor, and I see that he is pained by the same question that we all come back to: *Why do right and wrong look so similar?* Marvin gets up, like Ozymandias remounting his pedestal. He says,

'I don't want to pressure you, Harry. I know I bring a lot of pressure with me, just by being me.'

And he smiles, and we connect. He is enough of an amateur psychologist to have worked out that I had already thought that this was a shake-down in which I agreed to hide drug money in what looked like a charitable institution. But everything about the man tells me that is not the answer, nor anywhere near. He says,

'I'll be off. Think about it, will you? I did some bad things getting that money. If I could turn it into something good, it might even out. I don't know if that is how it works.'

'Marvin? We don't even know what "it" is.'

And the behemoth leaves Vanikin to his thoughts. This is a time of strangeness and mystery. I have become so glued to my existence, so hypnotised by routine, trick-ponied by my world of small concerns. And then, change. And then, another knock on the door. It is Estrella. She sits. I say,

'What's going on?'

'I don't know what you mean.'

'That's what they say in films, Estrella. Everyone is acting as though they have been given a new script.'

'Perhaps they have.'

'You see? The whole place has become a three-dimensional cryptic crossword.'

'Should be able to solve it, then, shouldn't you? Being an egghead.'

'I have seen all sorts of people acting strangely. Is there a full moon?'

'People like who?'

'Pilkington, the writer. Mr. Pilkington. Downstairs. Simon Pilkington, as a matter of fact.'

'Oh? What did he want?'

'For me to tutor him.'

'Ah. He doesn't like crowded places.'

'Don't expect me to look surprised. I know you know because he said he was going to talk to you.'

'About what?'

'Recordings. From the school.'

'Oh, that. He did that last week.'

'Well, then, why did he...? Never mind! He wants me to tutor him in, well, in a particular subject.'

'Do I have to guess? Is it a game? How many syllables? Sounds like?'

I look at my hands and then at the ceiling then hands again — ceiling, clock, and Estrella. Don't think I missed anything out. I say,

'My book. My own book. I haven't read my own book in seven years. Haven't even looked at it.'

'You don't have a copy?'

'No.'

'Not even an old manuscript.'

'No. No parchment copy or wax cylinder of me reciting the book at the British Library, either.'

'Oh well. Never mind. Happy birthday!'

I am now assuming that this is one of those top-of-the-range dreams, the ones that really do fool you with their special effects. I say,

'Estrella. If you are trying to drive me insane, you are succeeding. You are very, very good at it.'

'You are still on the website at the university. That's how I knew it was your birthday. Aries. Actually, I don't know anything about star-signs. I think it's all bollocks. Tomorrow afternoon's class on World War I is postponed, by the way. You can't make it. You're busy.'

Estrella, in addition to her surreal pronouncement, has produced a gift, wrapped tastefully in heavy brown paper and crisscrossed with a burgundy ribbon. It is certainly neither a jumper nor a bottle of scotch. She says,

'Don't read it all at once.'

And she is gone. I set the parcel on the table. The birthday boy. A memory from the past, flashing by like a train. My birthday, little Harry. Nadia and me at the table. Bright cone hats held on by chin-elastic. A mechanical tin robot who could fall off the table and not break. A diablo cup-and-ball. Tablets Nadia had which you dropped in water, and they turned into lily-pads. A flicker-book. Spirograph and a doll which talked. I pick up the parcel and slip off the ribbon without untying the knot. I peel back Sellotape carefully, carefully. Mother used to keep wrapping paper. I learned to coax sticky tape, not tear. When the trappings are loosed, I unfold the paper and look at the volume inside, which is brand new. I am familiar with the book, but not with this edition. On an impulse, I open it to the publisher's page and discover that it was published six months ago. It is always nice to have something to read. I close the book and look again at the cover, the fetching font and pleasing dusky green of the overall design. The cover says,

THE DECADENT TURN
THE LONG TWILIGHT OF ACADEMIC STUDY

PROFESSOR HARRY VANIKIN

CHAPTER TWENTY-FOUR

The Book of the Dead

If we ever walk the rooms, in memory, of a childhood home, we are there and not there. Physically, of course, we still live and breathe and have our being. There we are, there we stand, we can do no more. But our memories now clothe us, like a costume from a dressing-up box on a rainy day, when the adults have gone into town for important things. We are elsewhere. I am everywhere else.

Memories. The things you remember. Where were they the second before you recalled them? 'In a place,' writes Saint Augustine, 'which is as yet no place.' But memory is also about the things you *don't* remember. I don't, for example, remember an edition of my book from this particular publishing house, possibly the most famous academic imprint in Britain.

What I do remember is that my book was the culmination of two papers and a conversation in a bar in Montmartre with my dead wife. Dead now, I mean. Not then. The first paper was entitled *Denaissance: Philosophy and the Curriculum*, the second *Storming the Ivory Towers: Anti-Intellectualism and Communism*. That conversation, we will return to.

Both papers were non-specialist, what Clara used to call 'broad-brush' arguments. The first paper lamented the decline of philosophy as other disciplines rather tended to benefit from the advance of the modern technological world, while it didn't have much to offer to philosophy. A virtual library of British empiricism sounds great. You still have to read the British empiricists, though, and you may as well do that with a grubby Everyman copy of Hume or Locke which had once been used in a public-school book-cricket match. Probably a nicer read, I should think, but, then, I am morbidly afraid of computers and their ways.

The second paper was the one that turned out to be the blue touch-paper when the storm broke, if you will permit a mixed metaphor. It had so much of Clara in it I wanted to release the paper co-authored, but she gently resisted that. She said she knew a couple who did it, and the resultant reviews made the domestic air a little frigid for a while, as one author was favoured, the other not so much.

So, I published it under my name in *Philosophy and Politics*, and a twig never broke in the forest. It was only later, after the fireworks, that a twenty-two-year-old redbrick gunslinger — a transexual named Marrs D. M'Kona — called the paper 'the new type of respectable colonialism, in which pampered white academics tell wiser administrations how their domestic education policy should be run.'

How is it possible to deny that authoritarian regimes of the twentieth century went after intellectuals, Mao's purveyors of 'dangerous ideas'? It isn't. But what I didn't know then is that a generation of students were about to issue a general pardon to Communism. I mean, what's one hundred million dead souls between friends?

The conversation was, of course, with Clara. We had gone to Paris for a conference, and she took me to a favourite bar of hers by the *Sacré-Coeur*. She said,

'What's it going to be about?'

'What's what going to be about?'

'The book. The book you are going to write.'

'What makes you think I am going to write a book.'

She mimicked me saying that sentence and said it in the exact cadence and rhythm I used.

Now, on my beaten-up throne, like some Bohemian monarch, I read *The Decadent Turn* all night, fortifying myself with coffee and a couple of glasses of brandy. I know. It's like The Moulin Rouge here now. I don't have to read from scratch, as it were, of course. Some passages, I can glide through as they are sodden with familiarity. I wrote the bloody thing, after all.

It is, of course, what those saucy deconstructionists would have called a 'dual reading,' part conceptual and part flooded with the riptide of memory. Taking time off from particularly tricky passages to play chess with Clara. The British Library, raining outside and everyone's coats smelling warm and damp. Reading Adler and Schopenhauer and Lewis Carroll in Penny Black's café, Penny herself laughing when she saw me reading *Through the Looking-Glass, and What Alice Found There.* The occasional Vanikin tear, little salty globule, rolls down the saggy old cheeks as the clock ticks on and I turn the pages of the past.

And, finally, I lay the book aside. 'The end of all our exploration shall be to arrive where we started, and know the place for the first time.' T. S. Eliot, with his smart collars and his fascist fascinations. I had written an elegy, an encomium at a funeral, an ode to the departed. All I had wanted to do was mourn philosophy's passing by noting its gradual disappearance as the core of Western academic studies. How did I turn into Pol Pot? I need porridge.

Despite my entry into the marble halls of the gourmand in recent months — Estrella has even taught me to cook some rudimentary bachelor-fodder of my own — I still insist on porridge for breakfast. As I assemble the ingredients, I realise that I still don't have any shopping. What happened yesterday? What rent the veil of my routine? I investigate the depths of the cupboard and discover a few tins, refugees from the pre-

Epicurean days of yore. Tinned mandarins, SPAM, baked beans, baked beans with little sausages in, oxtail soup. I would make it through the day without requiring an air-drop from the United Nations.

Eating my porridge ruminatively, I once more try to join the dots the last two days have presented me with. Either there is something afoot, which is why everyone is behaving as though this is some children's party game, or I am paranoid for reasons that require diligent research, or I've just gone bonkers again. Not sure which I prefer.

Spooning my porridge into the good bowl, I begin to think of the first time I met Estrella. The days that followed, the weeks that became months. She was always the same: dispirited, lonely, seemingly longing to escape a cage that was neither gilded nor comfortable, but unable to grasp the details of and, therefore, the remedy for her plight. I suppose, if I am honest injun with myself, I helped bring her out of a shell which was becoming Silurian with age. And yet, now, without her to guide me through the underworld, I am stuck here like Ulysses in Calypso's cave. Which is on the little island off Malta, since you ask; I forget its name. Clara and I went there once, on bicycles. It was closed and covered in scaffolding. Calypso's cave, I mean, not the little island off Malta.

It is ten o'clock. Not only has Estrella not put in an appearance, no one else has, either. Oh, Christ. There hasn't been a nuclear war or a day of the triffids or an alien invasion or something, has there, and I missed it because I was asleep? Someone has usually beaten a path across the moors to see old man Vanikin by now. Is it Christmas? No. We had Christmas, months ago. Is it a plague, divine retribution, am I the last man on earth, like Charlton Heston in *The Omega Man*, or the last man in Europe, which is what Orwell was going to call *1984*, or just the last turkey in the shop? I make tea.

Vanikin, alone in the underworld. I may seem like a hermit, but a day has not gone by in the seven years and whatever tally Nadia has during which I have not had company of some sort. Lars and his newspaper, Declan and his roguish jive, Mrs. Podolski and her precision of language, Marek and his Polish lager, Mrs. Pallis and the kingdom of God, even Craig in the old days, with his reminders of the vagaries of human evolution. Magda with her book of spells, and Marvin M. and his hats. Just for one of them to visit now, just for a few seconds, I would give much.

I have no telephone. I have no computer. I have no television or radio. I elected to come down to the underworld, pull up all the ladders behind me and bury and burn all the maps that led here, and now look! A pretty pickle, Vanikin alone, vanquished Vanikin, whom no man knoweth.

What about Pilkington, the writer? Perhaps I could bang on the ceiling in morse code and tell him I am ready for his first lesson, having read the book, my own book, the core text. Maybe I could stand naked at the window until the police are called, and at least one of the neighbours will have to come round. No. The people of the overworld would just think it was performance art.

I recall the time I was snowed in at my first campus. I saw no one for four days. But I was younger then. Now, in the underworld, I have come to require the reciprocity of visitation. Even the guru, the village shaman, just wants sheer company and a good natter from time to time.

Time. It is midday. How do I even know my lesson is on? My fellow inmates may be being rounded up by some hideous authoritarian *Polizei*, and I wouldn't know. Where is the boy? Where is everyone, anyone? I make more tea and brood. I consider eating SPAM dipped in Oxtail soup. That will teach them.

The clock ticks mercilessly on like the blade in Poe's *The Pit and the Pendulum*. Well, a good deal less likely to bother a Health & Safety officer, I concede. 1:00 p.m. 1:15. 1:27. This is ridiculous, absurd. This is Ionesco and Beckett and Kafka rolled into one. Then, I remember the stabilisers, the little bicycle my father bought me, the excitement when the stabilisers are finally taken off, and it is up to you to provide the impetus and acceleration to stop the bicycle from toppling...

It is 1:50 p.m., and my lesson on World War I is due to begin in ten minutes, and no one has come for me, and I suddenly understand today's lesson. I gather my notes, place them in my dinky little briefcase — another of Estrella's purchases at the Aladdin's cave of the local charity shop, who I now practically sponsor — adjust my sunglasses, and leave the apartment unaccompanied for the first time in the recorded history of Europa House.

Where is everyone? Not everyone goes to my lessons, and Estrella and I would, in the normal course of things, encounter at least someone on the walkways, the stairwell, the courtyard. But the place is deserted. It's like a zombie movie before the zombies put in an appearance. I go to the games room. I have nowhere else to go.

I push open the door and go inside. The chairs are there, but their positions have been altered; now, they face towards the door, flanked down either side of the games room. They are fully occupied. Some folk are even standing. At the other end of the room is a podium. On the podium stand my sister, an unknown man, Roger Perrett, Simon Pilkington, an unknown man, an unknown man, Estrella, an unknown woman, Marvin M., and Dr. Benison. On the chairs, on either side of me as I walk mechanically towards the podium, unsure and Cartesian about whether this is or is not a dream, is, I believe and think I am right in saying, everyone else from Europa House. The applause begins modestly, and builds with an even pace until it sounds as though a thousand firecrackers are jumping around in the space and light.

CHAPTER TWENTY-FIVE

The Dinner Party

Dinner for the ten of us is most enjoyable, and so it should be because it is bloody expensive. I should know. I'm paying. I have a crab-and-mussel starter, beef stroganoff, and some French *broby* cheese to finish. I then have coffee and brandy. Let us review my guests' choice and then consider what they have to say for themselves, prior to our dinner engagement, concerning my situation. Let us begin, as is only right and proper, with my sister Nadia.

She has a starter of French toast with curried taramasalata, a main course of haunch of venison with haricot beans, onion marmalade, and mashed parsnip, and a chocolate mousse for dessert. She loved chocolate as a child, often looking at a bar of unwrapped chocolate she had bought for as long as she possibly could before consuming it. Here is a snippet from our earlier conversation:

'I couldn't tell you, Harry. No one could. Some of the papers you signed were the contract. If we had told you, you might never have come out.'

Dr. Mark Benison, now my personal physician, has a clear shrimp soup, I think followed by a good old-fashioned steak — what we used to call a 'Tom and Jerry steak' — and sorbet to follow. He joins me for the brandy course, putting in sterling work on the fine bottle we (I) purchase. This is the good doctor's contribution to proceedings:

'Nothing wrong with you physically, but if anyone had told you that you would be going outdoors, you would have collapsed into illness. It's what agoraphobics do. Their anxiety is so great that if all the barriers are removed to leaving the house, they will develop a range of psychosomatic illnesses to make that impossible. So, we all had to, sort of, I don't know, work you up to it. Everyone was in on it. I'm not a psychiatrist, by the way, I just used to fuck someone who was.'

Marvin M. renounces a starter and heads straight for a rack of ribs, a meal the menu proudly announces is sufficient to feed four people. Marvin also foregoes dessert and any type of cheese, coffee, or alcohol, being actually quite abstemious apart from his food consumption and, as one might expect, the inhalation of prodigious quantities of strong cannabis. Marvin quoth thus:

'Professor, Harry. I know that you don't need the money now, but I still want to make it available. It means a lot to me. I never went to school except to deal drugs and get an alibi. And I know you think I want to launder the money. I don't. Even if I did, then a lot of money is laundered. A lot of money, a *lot* of money, that looks clean and fresh and nice is made by bad people.'

The unfamiliar young lady, as it transpires, is Estrella's oft-mentioned accomplice, Sarah. Now, she has sushi, with that very hot Japanese paste the name of which escapes me, then a poached salmon with another Japanese concoction which looks like, and almost certainly is, seaweed which has been put through its paces by wily Oriental culinary alchemy, although this paradigm of health on a plate comes to an abrupt end when she orders chocolate gateau. She has a decaffeinated coffee and a glass of Cointreau, which I find delightful. Her two pennies' worth:

'I don't think it will be all that much more difficult than

being an ordinary secretary. Or having a little brother. I've done both. We'll meet Monday, if that's okay?'

One of the unknown men actually is known to me. I just haven't seen him for over seven years and don't recognise him. His name is Patrick Coburn, and he had been — and still is — an administrator at my university. He dines on a very simplistic avocado salad as a starter, lamb cutlets for main, sorbet for dessert, and a dessert wine, a Tokay, which meant nothing to me at the time but which I have since found is rather grand and Prussian. Here is his news:

'I think, if you agree, we would like a sort of, I don't know, re-inaugural lecture? Date of your choosing, of course.'

Simon Pilkington has smoked salmon to start, over which he squeezes a lime with the finality of an all-in wrestler, and then mills pepper over the result, strafing the fish with small black full-stops and commas, as befits a writer. For his main course, he has pasta penne with pesto, and braised red peppers, and then opts for the complementary chocolates everyone else doesn't want, and many coffees. He had had a word earlier in my shell-like ear:

'It wasn't just that I had to get you to read it again. I really have read it five times. I was just in the right place at the right time. Sarah would like me to write your biography. If that's okay with you, Harry. We were thinking of calling it *Vanikin in the Underworld*. What do you think? Is it too? Too? What do the Americans say? Hoaky?'

One of the unknown men is named Stanford Caul, a literary agent, and he is, he tells me, half-American and half-Australian. He has soup to start, but I am not sure which soup, a full crab on the shell — must be the Australian in him — and ice cream, before joining the good doctor and I for brandy. We have entered into a professional relationship. In conversation to confirm this, he said earlier:

'That doctor chap's nice. And he says you would have no problem doing a lecture tour. There is none of that de-platforming crap anymore. That was one of the first things to go. We could even get you an American tour.'

Roger Perrett, aka the measuring man, is not Roger Perrett at all but Dominic Kent, and he really does write for a major national newspaper. He is the journalist Estrella told me would be coming. He tucks into whitebait as a *commencer*, moves swiftly along to pork medallions with fennel salad, makes light work of some sort of cake, and is another enthusiastic member of our brandy symposium. He confessed thus:

'I didn't feel good about lying to you. Can you believe that? A journalist uncomfortable about lying! But I wanted the story to develop, and I didn't want to hit you with it all at once. We're going to serialise. That will be another little earner for you. Well, you've got staff to pay now.'

Estrella is a little duplicitous also, it transpires, and was in on this monstrous, *grand guignol* academic enterprise a lot earlier than my recollections would suggest. She has little meatballs, tiny *mazzos*, as a starter, demolishes a seafood carbonara, glides through butterscotch tart, and finishes with coffee and Armagnac. We really are boulevardiers now; we've arrived. Her story ran like this:

'We all did our bit. It wasn't just me. If you had come out to find all this without finding your feet first, you would have run straight back into your room again. The book is doing so well, we had to shield you from it or you would have freaked out. Freaked out! I can't believe I said that! That is how I used to talk when I was about fourteen!'

The final puzzle-piece turns out to the managing director of Britain's largest academic publishing house, as noted in a previous episode. Peter Renford dines simply, claiming suspect digestion, with a hake pâté to kick off, an impressive Waldorf salad, sorbet, and a decaf coffee. He really is quite a bigwig and has startling news:

'Once the walls came tumbling down, as it were, on the old woke culture, yours was one of the first titles that started to shift units. A couple of journos — Dominic was one — championed you and *The Decadent Turn* as one of the most innocent victims of the culture wars, and, well, it was like those records that get criticism then everyone buys it, and it goes to number one at Christmas. You've been number one in the academic best-seller list for over a year and number four in the all-comers list. You're worth well over a million pounds. And counting.'

I have the waiter pour me another brandy.

It is later now, after the festivities, and I am sitting on my throne for the last time. I requested one more night in the old homestead, one last rumination in the underworld before the fierce glamour of the overworld claims me, Orpheus *redux*.

The scale of the deception, of course, was almost governmental. Under the medical tutelage of Dr. Benison — Mark, I should say — the cast performed their parts impeccably, preparing old man Vanikin, setting up the return of the king. They are all correct. I would never have gone out without, as it were, due process. But going out, I am.

Craig has arranged for a 'man with a van' to pick up my personal effects. He actually talked of a 'manwivan,' making his acquaintance sound like a pretty coastal town in Wales. These things will be delivered to my new dwelling, which my sister bought outright and which I have visited. It is in a leafy and quaint part of what remains of old London, and I am very happy with it. Doesn't matter if you're not, said Nadia. We'll just buy another one. Things, I am reliably informed, have changed rather since I was last out.

It started, so the nibs tell me, with a new government. The

old one had been voted out, it transpired, largely because there were still enough sane, ordinary people who just were not going to put up with there being sixty or so genders, an almost entirely fabricated history of slavery, a moratorium on the nuclear family, a ban on Christmas, endless uncontrolled immigration, and the various other replacement mythologies with which the radical Left-wing had infested society. So, democracy won, and Vanikin was a prime beneficiary.

And so, Vanikin remained deep in the belly of Europa House, unaware that the world was searching for him. He crept about like the apocryphal Japanese soldiers in the jungles of Asia, unaware that the war had ended and only emerging, blinking in the light, years after VE Day. Of course, they would also have learned about VJ Day, whereas Vanikin is going out not into a world of defeat and shame and loss of face, but of laurels and fine wine and the imperial purple. To the Vanikin, the spoils.

I look around the old place. My cave, my cell, my empire, won with difficulty but ruled with ease and clemency. I have my small briefcase at the ready. I line it with an old shirt — Sarah is, apparently and rather frighteningly, already working on my new wardrobe — and in it, I place my clock. When I leave, I will be taking time with me, and I have a slightly uncanny feeling — *unheimlich*, old Nietzsche would have called it — that my life is somehow intimately and inexorably bound with the destiny of the clock. We both languished at the back of the shop until someone bought us.

I take a last look out of the window, blacked out by my own artificial night for so many years, and I take a last look at the Gyproc partition, the winded and wounded sofa, my throne, abdicated now. One last look at the underworld, the land of the shades, the other side of the River Styx. Then, I open the door and go outside.

Further Reading
from the Good People at
Falling Marbles Press

NOT JUST A JOB
by Michael Long

A quartermaster's naval misadventure,
as served in the 1970s West Pacific

"The Navy. It's not just a job, it's an
adventure." So said the television ads,
and so, having graduated high-school
during America's withdrawal from
Vietnam, Gary Thorpe signed up. A
quartermaster, his job is to steer and
navigate the ship, but he learns quickly
that being in the US Navy entails much
more – as well as much less – than
advertised.
Not Just A Job is sure to relate to anyone who has ever found himself
in a situation less than he imagined.

RAVENS ON A WIRE
by Andrew Bacevich

Vietnam's dark legacy, as faced on
the West German border

The first novel from noted historian
and author of over a dozen books,
Andrew Bacevich, *Ravens on a Wire*
chronicles a routine border incident
and its subsequent investigation, during
which the wounds of Vietnam find
themselves on the verge of being
reopened. For some, the regiment's
motto – "Duty, with Honor" – would
seem to demand this reopening, no matter how painful the results.

Further Reading
from the Good People at
Falling Marbles Press

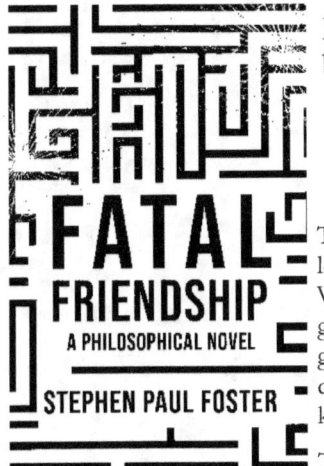

FATAL FRIENDSHIP
by Stephen Paul Foster

The age-old Rousseau-Hobbes
debate solved, merely requiring
a grisly murder (or two)

The novel begins when Frank Bradley learns that his best friend, Rich Wahnfried, has brutally murdered his girlfriend. The ghastly news that his good friend was a closeted monster detonates Frank's confidence that he knows anyone, starting with himself.

This philosophical novel, authored by a preeminent interpreter of the human soul, follows the path to understanding the darkness in the human condition.

Falling Marbles

Check out the Falling Marbles website for
all current and upcoming titles

www.fallingmarbles.com